DARED TO RETURN

J. J. Clarke

DARED TO RETURN

A Kate Anderson Mystery

J. J. CLARKE

This novel is a work of fiction. Characters, organizations, names and events are a product of the author's imagination or are used fictionally.

The one exception is Chariton County, Missouri. It is an actual place and holds a special place in my heart.

Printed in the United States of America

ISBN: 9781795463942

DEDICATION

To Barry William, my co-conspirator and creator
in our wonderful adventure

ACKNOWLEDGEMENTS

I want to thank my family, especially my husband, for listening to my endless stories about the manuscript.

Thank you to my writer's groups—The Writers of the Villages, the Working Writer's Group and the Snow Bird Internet Group. Without their critiques and cheerleading, this novel would be in the bottom of the closet.

Thank you to my Beta Readers and their kind comments and suggestions.

A special thank you to My Circle of Friends Golf Group who cheered me on every step of the way.

Thank you, Bona Hayes, who put the sparkle in my pages. She read and reread the manuscript with glee, making corrections. The best of luck on your new business!

We owe our wonderful cover design, a hometown setting with overtones of danger, to the creative talents of Josh Lucchesi.

And for capturing the storm on the cover, kudos to Matthew Anderson at Andersonphotography.com.

TABLE OF CONTENTS

*The only thing necessary for the triumph of evil
is for good men to do nothing.*

--Edmund Burke

PROLOGUE

I thought she was dead. The coughing had stopped, and she lay still. Helen Anderson's delicate blue veins in her hands collapsed as I stood and watched. Diamond rings, surrounded in gold and on every finger, stood out in contrast to the white sheet and blue veins. Her perfectly polished nails—pearl colored—were turned to a shade of grey.

Her husband Theodore had stood vigil by the woman's side most of the last three days, talking to her and saying his rosary. Now he lay exhausted, reclined in the hospital chair by the window. He snored, his glasses askew. His white hair, usually combed neatly, stood up on end. They had been in hospice care for five days.

By now, I'm used to death, being a hospice nurse, but this couple I knew. Everyone knew who they were—they had given jobs to half the people in town. When I was a little girl, I tried to sneak a candy bar out of their store. My mother, mortified, made me apologize.

Tears welled in my eyes as I looked down at her. *I should hold her hand.* As I reached down to check her pulse, her steel blue eyes blinked open at me. I gasped as she said, "I never wanted that charity foundation, I never wanted that trust."

Her head fell to the side.

Theodore Anderson sat straight up and leapt from the chair.

"She's gone, I know she's gone." His legs buckled as he tried to hobble to her side.

He grabbed her hand, kissed it, then stood by her bed and cried.

—HQ, August 04, 2015

CHAPTER ONE

POPS

Tampa, Florida, September 2015, 11:30 pm

Kate Anderson's phone buzzed. She stopped pedaling the elliptical in the Anytime Fitness Center. The machine slowed to a stop and she glanced at her watch.

"Pops, is that you?"

"Katrina, Oh, Katrina, thank goodness I reached you — please come home."

"What's wrong, Pops? You never call me this late." Kate stepped off the machine, crossed the gym floor, wiped her forehead with a towel and strained to hear her grandfather's voice.

"Katrina, I don't want to stay here."

Kate pushed open the locker room door and froze. A cold chill crept down her spine and crawled up her forearms.

"Where are you, Grandpa? What's wrong?"

"I'm at Squaw Valley Nursing Home. They moved me here."

"What — I mean, who? Grandpa, who moved you there? Why aren't you home? Are you ill?"

"No, no, I'm not sick — that trustee. I can't remember his name — it doesn't matter. I must go. They are looking for me. Please come home, Katrina."

"Pops!" Katrina heard the click on the other end of the line and stared at her phone. Kate immediately hit redial. He did not answer. *Who can I call? Surely, there's someone I can call.* She wiped imaginary sweat from her brow.

What's happened since Grandma's funeral? How has he gone from their home to a nursing home in just four or five weeks? Kate pressed the travel app on her phone, booked a flight, a rental car and a hotel. *When was the last time I talked to him? Grandma's funeral? How long has it been since the funeral, four, five weeks? How can he be in a nursing home? Trustee, what trustee?*

Kate reached up and felt her cheeks as they flushed in anger. *This can't be happening. I just want to scream!* Kate's relationship with her grandfather had always been strained, but family duty trumped everything.

Kate jogged down the steps, out of the gym and to her car. She cursed that she had parked at the far end of the parking lot underneath the light. Her red Mazda's lights blinked a few seconds before she arrived. She slid into the driver's seat, started the engine and then sped through town, blowing a few stop signs.

Kate arrived at her luxury one-bedroom apartment overlooking Tampa Bay. She grabbed a suitcase from the closet and packed a few clothes. Cosmetics and hair clips laid neatly lined up in the drawer and ready to be put into her cosmetic bag. Years of practice paid off—and the items flew into her case. *Still on the run.* The irony played on the corner of her mouth and she smiled, loving the adrenaline. Once at the airport, she fired a text to her friend and publicist.

Hey girl, jetting out tonight.
Pops needs me.
Reschedule my book club signings.
Gotta run to catch a flight.
Kate.

A text bubble burst onto Kate's phone.
Oh, no you don't. Not this time.
Text me the details. I'll meet you there.

∽ ∽ ∽

Will Johnson, the plane's steward, waited for the remaining passenger to board. Why can't people just get on the damn plane? It looks like another boring flight. He looked at his watch. His last passenger had another two minutes. He saw her walking up the ramp, dressed in designer jeans and a leather jacket. Her long brown hair, braided French style, pulled away from the face. She wore tall expensive leather boots and walked like a model. She carried a large Coach handbag. When she reached him, she gave him her ticket.

"Good evening, Ms. Anderson. I'm glad you made it. My name is Will and I'm your attendant. Your seat is the first one on the left."

"First-class, I like it." Kate tossed her bag into the compartment and crumpled into the first seat across from where the steward sits facing the passengers. She buckled her seatbelt. The plane was warm and dark. She reached up to add air from the port above her seat and wriggled out of her coat.

Will walked the aisle, checked passengers' seat belts and closed overhead compartments. *Wow. My night just got more interesting.*

Most passengers were settling in for the night flight nap. The plane was only half full and dimly lit. He returned to his little jump-seat facing Kate and buckled himself.

"I've been drinking," Kate announced. "I always say that when I've had one too many." She laughed and shook her head. "I sped all the way here, well I always speed. I didn't know they had those little convenience stores with alcohol."

Will leaned toward the beautiful woman. "You're not afraid of flying? It's the safest transportation."

"I'm not afraid." Kate massaged the palms of her hands and then her fingers. "It's more like dreadful memories. My parents were killed in a plane crash when I was four."

"No— now you're kidding, right?"

"My father piloted the plane carrying the newly elected U.S. Senator, my small town's claim to fame. It crashed at the airport in Kingseat, Missouri."

"Wow, yes, flying must be hard, but your ticket was changed to first-class, so you must fly often."

"No, my business partner is a frequent flyer. I'm sure she changed my ticket." Kate held her breath as the plane released the brakes and started down the runway.

"You know the best thing for you to do is to take big breaths — and let's talk — it will be a good diversion."

"Sounds good — talk, Will. Tell me your story. I'm a writer in desperate need of a new story." Kate closed her eyes for a moment. *I wonder if my mother was terrified the night she died.*

"Don't go to sleep, Kate. Yes, I'll tell you my story."

Kate opened her eyes and studied the young man. "How old are you, Will?"

"I remember the story of your parent's plane crash, so I am a few years older than you, thirty-two. I'm a licensed engineer -- graduated six years ago from the University of Missouri. I'm working on my master's in business. I applied for this job right out of college as a lark. I love to fly — I wanted to be a pilot — but my depth perception is poor. I am, however, the exact right height to close these bins." He pointed upward and shot her a little grin. "The job gives me a great deal of freedom and — and at least I might have adventures to tell my grandchildren someday. Right now, I fly Tampa to Kansas City and live in K.C."

The plane began the ascent and Kate grabbed the arms of her chair.

"It's really okay. Anyway, that's my life story — *Cliff* note style. Tell me more about yourself. When the seat belt sign goes off, I'll get you another drink."

Kate readjusted in her seat and took a deep breath. "Let me see, my story-- well, it's a little complicated. I grew up in Kingseat, Missouri, raised by my grandfather, step grandmother and a nanny — a sweet Amish lady. It took all of them, I was a wild child. I went to Catholic school, graduated from college with a law enforcement degree, worked as a bond investigator until five years ago. I planned to go to law school, but instead— fled after becoming the prime suspect in a murder investigation.

Will sat up taller in his seat, his mouth fell open and he stared at the woman sitting across from him. He managed to say, "This time you *are* joking?"

Kate grinned. "Oh, that margarita really loosened my tongue. I wish I were joking. A warrant was issued for my arrest and instead of turning myself in and sitting in jail convicted of a crime I didn't commit, I kept moving, barely a step ahead of the U.S. Marshall's Office." Kate shrugged her shoulders. "No big deal really. Like you said—adventures to tell the grandchildren."

"You aren't on the run now, are you?" Will asked with a crooked little smile.

Kate did not return his smile, but instead looked out the window. Suddenly she turned and brightened, lighting up the dark plane. "No, crazy, I couldn't fly if I had a warrant out for me."

"You should write a book."

"I did. It's called *Dared to Run*, not exactly a best seller, but we have a marketing plan. I work a few private investigations and write articles for blogs and a few newspapers. Like you said, it works for me. Oh, and—my partner is a pretty successful Youtuber."

"Wow, what kind of Vlog? Business partner, right? Not partner, like in a relationship partner."

"It's based on the 1920's gentlemen's club entertainment, just a little burlesque show, you know — beautiful women, great bodies, a little skit making fun of modern times, and a little skin. We say we are artsy, not nudey. It's a little risqué. Susie's the star–I write the skits."

"I keep saying, you're joking, right?"

"No, that's me. Condensed version. Oh, yes, I'm single."

Will got up and pointed toward the front deck. "I need to make sure my partner has the bar cart. She'll cover for me. Hold your thought, we're not done. Can I get you something? A drink, pretzels, chips?"

"Water, please, coffee later. I have a long drive when we land."

Will returned to his seat across from Kate. She was busy making notes in a small spiral notebook.

"Almost everyone's asleep, so I can talk. Kate, do you live in Tampa?"

"Yes, I love it here. I'm flying in to Missouri to check on my grandfather. He asked me to come home, so here I am, on a plane. It might turn into an extended stay. I feel guilty." Kate stopped herself and shook her head. "Why am I telling you this? You probably didn't want to hear my confession."

"You have my full attention, confess away."

"My grandmother died about five weeks ago. I should have stayed after the funeral. I've been busy promoting my book, building a new life for myself. Now that I think about it, my grandfather was pushing me out the door, hiding something. I should have known better."

Kate shifted in her seat. "Let's change the subject. Do you know you look like JFK?"

"Of course, people tell me that all the time." Will laughed at himself. "I'm joking. Well, a couple of times. Once, a woman said to me, 'are you Jack Kennedy?' The two laughed. "I don't know what she was thinking," Will said.

He cocked his head at Kate. "You look like…hmm … I don't know, this might get me in trouble."

"I'll help you out, this is my standard 'Sandra Bullock, don't approach me' look. Do you see it?"

"I spotted it immediately when you were coming up the ramp, not so much now."

"My friends know I'm much like her character in Miss Congeniality."

The two laughed and whispered secrets in the darkness, creating their own private world until it was time to land. When the plane started its descent, Will moved over next to Kate and held her hand. She placed her head on his shoulder and closed her eyes.

CHAPTER TWO

CONSTRUCTION

Kingseat, Missouri   7:00 a.m.

Kate Anderson parked the SUV a short block from her grandfather's house. A construction sign prevented her from driving into his cul-de-sac. Forms for a new porch were in place; the beautiful brick porch, which once stood so stately, was now destroyed.

She studied the situation for a few moments. Her heart raced and she took a deep breath. *What the 'F' is going on?* She gasped as if surfacing after being trapped underwater. Of all the things she thought would never change, it was the front porch of this beautifully designed home. Kate's stomach rolled and heaved as a memory caught her like a fly in a spider web. She could see herself as a tiny girl playing with dolls, singing songs about mommy and daddy, the doggie, waiting for her parents who never came home.

Kate steadied her nerves by studying the crew and the new construction. Having spent so much time in tactical maneuvers, she admired the efficient teamwork. She wiped a tear from her eye, jogged the short distance down the street and maneuvered the maze of bricks, boards, rebar and stones.

"Big project you have going here," Kate shouted over the noise of the jackhammers.

"Yes, it is."

"Good crew you've got running." Kate managed a smile.

"Yes, tis," he pointed to the garage, and they both stepped in. "Can I help you with something?"

"I hope so. I'm Kate Anderson, can you tell me who owns this place? My grandfather built it—I've been gone—and I heard it had…"

He turned before Kate finished her sentence and walked to the inside door of the house. A tall, older man wearing jeans and a sweatshirt answered the door.

"Good morning, Mr. Roush, I hope we didn't start too early for you," the foreman said to the older gentlemen.

"No, Clayton, I was just thinking about checking on you. Do you have time for a cup of coffee?"

"No sir, not now. You have a visitor. This here is Kate Anderson. She's Theodore Anderson's granddaughter. She came for a visit this morning."

Kate stepped up to shake the man's hand. She smiled at Clayton. Introductions in small towns helped put people at ease. It's a bond of trust, not easily obtained.

"Come in, come in, Ms. Anderson," the older man said.

"Please call me Kate." She followed him into the kitchen and looked around the room. Grandmother's table and hutch were pushed against the wall, covered in plastic. The chairs were lined against another wall. She stared at the open spaces where the stove and refrigerator once stood. All the carpet, drapes, and accessories were removed. Kate imagined her grandmother's treasures in the front yard, people milling through them.

"Wow!" Kate's hand covered her mouth in an involuntary gesture.

"This must be a shock for you."

"Well, yes, but that's not why I'm here. I wanted to know if you had any questions—about the house, or if there is anything I could do to help." The two stood awkwardly in the kitchen. She remained quiet as she fought images of throwing things.

"Cup of coffee?"

"Yes, please," Kate answered.

Mr. Roush offered Kate a folding chair and grabbed one for himself. The chairs flopped like wounded birds, as jackhammers droned outside. The noise added to Kate's heart racing and her mind spun in circles with questions.

"We bought this house fair and square," Roush said.

Kate sipped the black liquid, studying him over the rim of her cup. After a few seconds of the silent stand-off, Kate leaned in and said, "Would you mind telling me about the purchase? I'm confused."

14

"Well, it's all very simple. Your grandparents held an auction and sold most of their belongings. They kept some furniture for the assisted living apartment they were planning to move to. We bought these items," he gestured around the room, "and many more at the auction. Your grandfather showed us this place twice, and he was quite candid about how much money he wanted for it. I think there was one other serious bidder, but we met her price and outbid her."

I feel like I'm playing a game of high stakes poker. Wait, let him talk. Kate studied the man.

Roush looked down at his mug and swirled his coffee. "We've heard your grandfather didn't receive any money from the sale of the house, is this true?"

Kate crossed her legs, trying to remain calm and mimic the slow Missouri speech and body language. "I don't know, Mr. Roush, I have more questions than answers. I didn't even know they were considering assisted living. I'm not winning any granddaughter awards." Kate played the sympathy card.

"It's a brand-new place, called the Morning Glory Assisted Living Center, about a mile from here. Your grandparents loved this neighborhood so close to the church. Your granddad has not lived anywhere else for sixty some years." Roush smiled, "Your granddad gave me my first job. Those two gave half the people in this town their first chance. Is it true he's in Squaw Valley Nursing Home?"

Kate's hands trembled. She sat her cup on the counter, rubbed her hands together and blew on them

15

as if she were cold. "Not for long, I'm moving him today, if humanly possible." Kate stood up. "Before I leave, could I ask what closing agent you used?"

Roush rose, crossed the kitchen, opened a drawer and pulled out a stack of paperwork and handed it to her. "Your grandmother died before the closing," he volunteered. "The house was in your grandmother's trust. They gave me three copies, you can keep all that." Jim handed Kate the paperwork. "It shows the complete transaction from the auction to the closing. Your granddad's name was not on the title to the house."

Kate stood still as if someone just threw cold water in her face. After a few seconds she managed to say, "Thank you, Mr. Roush, this has been most helpful. I don't want to put you on the spot, but have you heard anything about the farms?"

Roush stood up and poured another cup of coffee. "Um…yes, but it's just gossip. You should talk to your grandmother's attorney."

"Of course, but who doesn't like a little gossip?" Kate flashed her winning smile.

"Coffee shop rumor says you inherited the fishing cabin. Your Uncle Bob's livid. I guess he thought he was her heir. You know— like your grandmother, your uncle has no biological heirs."

"I never thought about it, but I guess that's true. My father was not Grandma Helen's son. Uncle Bob doesn't have any children, either," Kate said.

"That's all I should say. Be careful. The farmhand who has been with your Uncle Bob for thirty some years is a real hot head."

"So am I." Kate laughed for the first time that morning. "It'll be fine. He's not really my uncle, I guess you knew that. I'm sorry, I'm just lost in thought about the reason I came." Kate pointed to the laundry room. "Did you find Grandfather's plans for the house?"

"No. He said there were architectural plans. We thought they would be here auction day, but we never found them."

Kate crossed the kitchen into the laundry and looked up at the cabinet over the space where the washer had once been. "I bet they're up on top."

Roush moved a step stool over. Kate climbed the stool and placed her hands on top of the cabinet, moving back-and-forth piano-playing style until she found the rolled architectural plans. She handed them to him and climbed down. "A little dusty."

Roush took the plans. "You've saved me a great deal of time."

Kate glanced at her watch. "I've gotta see Pops." She exited without the proper midwestern niceties at the door. She crossed the yard and jogged back down the street, jumped in her rental and sped away.

She did not look back.

CHAPTER THREE

SQUAW VALLEY

K ate Anderson sat in her rented SUV and pounded the steering wheel with the palms of her hands. *I just can't believe it. Squaw Valley Nursing Home of all places!* She exited the vehicle, locked her car, and strode up to the front door which was locked. *What is this, a prison?*

Kate pushed the button and a voice on the intercom stated, "May I help you?"

"I'm Kate Anderson. I'm here to see my grandfather, Theodore Anderson." Kate waited for a reply from the receptionist. She checked for cameras, applied some lip gloss and pushed the button again.

"I'm sorry, Ms. Anderson, you will have to come back later." The voice crackled, "Visiting hours are from two to four."

"What? Let me in. Let me in or I'll come back with a sledgehammer." Kate flushed with anger. She wondered if she could kick in the door. After hearing no immediate reply, she pushed the button again. "Let me in."

The door buzzed. Kate grabbed it and slung it open. The smells of the nursing home hit her in the face. *Calm down.* Disinfectant, sickness and bedpans identified, as she rubbed her nose and surveyed the room. *What is this room, just a parking lot for old people?* Most of the patients were dressed in hospital gowns, their eyes staring out into space. One woman rocked a doll baby and sang to it, while a man muttered, "Shut up!"

Kate searched for her grandfather. She turned to the nurses' station and counted four employees dressed in maroon scrub tops and tan pants. They studied charts and ignored everything else. Bells dinged while white lights on the switchboard blinked. None of the employees responded to the constant sound of unanswered calls for help.

This is no place for Pops. Could Grandfather be a ward of the Court? Could someone else be his guardian? Feeling sick, Kate looked around for a bathroom. It occurred to her the nurses were avoiding contact and the receptionist appeared extra busy. The news of Kate's arrival at the front door must have traveled down the hall to the administrator's office. Her stomach settled as she focused on her surroundings.

Kate caught a glimpse of a young woman dressed in a bright pink smock, her lipstick expertly applied, hair neat and sprayed. A bright, toothy smile spread across her made-up face.

"Katie, is that you?"

"Yes, I'm here to see my grandfather, Theodore Anderson." The nurse in the bright pink smock morphed into a younger version of herself. Kate recognized her from high school.

"Harriet Jones. Quinn now, I married Michael Quinn." Harriet extended her right hand to shake, waving her left hand, exposing the significant diamond on her ring finger.

"Oh hello, Harriet, good to see you."

"Kate, you look the same—tall, thin, beautiful. You are a natural. You still don't use much make up, do you? Like I said, you're just beautiful! I'm a trained *'Mary Kay'* consultant, if you ever want to doll up a bit. I could make you look like Sandra Bullock."

"Well thank you, Harriet. I'm in a hurry. Could you help me find my grandfather? We can catch up another time. *Am I being handled by an old high school acquaintance or am I paranoid?*

"Of course, Katie. But, you know, we have our rules." Harriet used the sing song speech saved for the elderly patients. "Let's go meet Mr. Carr."

Harriet led Kate down a series of hallways and chatted about her husband, their big church wedding and their little farm. Kate pretended she was interested in Harriet's life. She checked hallways and exits but kept her bearings through the twists and turns of the facility.

Small town etiquette…one listens to endless talk about other people's lives. It's only polite. Kate knew graduating high school together was significant in a small town. It bonded people together like serving in the Army or surviving a car crash.

"We just love your grandfather. He is such a nice, God-loving man. He makes a wonderful addition to our little family here. He truly has the patience of a saint."

Maybe he's not here. That's not the Pops I know.

Harriet escorted Kate into a small office with a desk and phone, adding machine and several ledgers. "Mr. Carr, our administrator, will be right with you. I will go and tell Theodore he has a visitor. He will be so glad to see you."

"Yes, he will be." Kate looked Harriet straight in the eye, all business. "What room is he in? I always like to know where I'm going."

"Of course you do, dear." Harriet turned and left the room.

Kate thought about confronting her but heard a man's voice in a nearby office. She strained to hear the conversation. The voice, low and controlled, disagreed with the party on the other end of the line.

"She's sitting in the office right now. You need to see her immediately." Kate heard the receiver slam down. She waited for a moment and returned to the hallway, found the bathroom and stepped in. She pulled out her phone and called her grandfather.

After several rings she heard him whisper, "Hello."

"Pops, I'm in the front office, what room are you in?"

"Katrina, oh, I'm so glad you're here. Do you want me to come down there?"

"I'll find you, what room are you in?"

After hearing 'room 35', Kate bolted from the bathroom and retraced her steps. She looked for a map on the wall or some reasoning in the maze of the nursing home.

She ran headlong into Harriett.

"Oh, Harriett, Mr. Carr appears to be busy. You know, I'm just gonna peek in on Pops, I'm so anxious to see him. Could you point me in the right direction, just blame it on me, Harriet?" Kate matched Harriet's sing-song tone but did not stop as she worked her way down the hallway looking left and right. She started to jog.

"Last door!" Harriet called out. Kate gave her a backwards prom wave as she sprinted down the hall.

Kate knocked on the door and entered. An old white-haired man sat in a dirty recliner. Kate almost didn't recognize him. A small television blared in the room. Unshaven, uncombed, wearing a hospital gown two sizes too large, her grandfather looked twenty years older than when she last saw him at her grandmother's funeral in his tailored black suit.

"Pops, what are you doing here?" She wrapped her arms around the thin, frail old man.

"Katrina, how did you get here so quickly? Did you fly, Katrina? Oh, you flew home for me."

"Yes, Pops, I flew home. I'm home, Pops, it's okay."

He struggled to get out of his recliner. Kate waited until he stood upright and kissed him on the cheek. The old man clung to the young woman, then reached for the arms of the chair and slowly sat back down. He covered his face with his withered hands and broke out into heart wrenching sobs.

"I may have lost everything."

CHAPTER FOUR

REUNION

Dirty *Sally's Tavern*, located at the edge of town, served good food and catered to a younger crowd. The bar consisted of one large room, bar in the middle, booths on the outside walls, pool tables in the back. Cigarette smoke filled the air. Regulars drank beer at the bar and early bird senior diners devoured the daily special—leftovers from lunch. The waitresses wore short shorts and low-cut jerseys.

Kingseat, Missouri, a proud river town, built by steamboat captains and later the railroad, held onto its proud heritage. Pictures of locals holding huge man-sized catfish hung on the bulletin board. A picture of the world's largest pecan statue and snapshots of kid's baseball teams decorated the walls. A mounted elk head looked over the cash register. He had seen better days.

Kate opened the door. "Uptight bitch!" a familiar voice echoed from the bar. Kate zeroed in on her friend, but let her eyes adjust to the darkness before taking another step.

"Sleazy Night Ho," Kate drawled as she cut across the restaurant in a few quick strides. The women hugged and rocked each other side to side, both decked out in skinny jeans and tall expensive boots. People stopped eating and drinking and stared at the two attractive women. A couple in the back whispered to each other. Kate could almost hear them say, "Not from around here."

Susie whistled for the bartender and pointed at her drink. "She'll have one of these."

The bartender nodded as he checked out the new girl in the room.

"You've already made a friend," Kate said.

"Sure, having a little fun. You look like you could use some! You okay?"

Kate's friend and publicist, Susie Jones, outgoing and dramatic, was the opposite of Kate. Susie, sometimes obnoxious, Kate usually guarded and polite. Five years ago, the two women worked together as court investigators, drawing a steady pay check from the State of Missouri. Now, they made a great team: Susie, a brilliant editor and researcher, Kate the imaginative writer.

"You look awful. What a pathetic mess you are. How's Pops?"

"Dressed, which is a big improvement—but he's mad as hell. He's in the room next to yours at the B&B. You share a wall. You might not want company tonight—waking him banging your head on the headboard."

"Outrageously cheeky, you are." Susie teased Kate in her very best British accent. "Wait—you broke him out of the nursing home? Pops wasn't dressed? I can't imagine Pops, being in that state. He's always so dapper."

"The nursing home refused to refund his month's rent. So, the stubborn old coot wanted to stay. I've flown in to help him—within minutes, we're fighting. 'We're staying in a palace,' according to him. I fought him and the director of the nursing home. It took all damn day." Kate looked around the room. "The problem with small towns, everyone has ears. Let's start by getting a booth and something to eat."

Susie blew a kiss to the bartender. They grabbed a booth by the pool tables and the back door.

"Before we get to Pops, I have some good news. No lawsuit!" Susie chimed in.

"What?"

"Reese Matthews signed the waiver allowing us to use his real name in your novel. And, get this. Yesterday, the mayor announced Matthews has been appointed Police Chief. Here, starting tomorrow." Susie made wild gestures ending with her finger pounding on the table.

"Oh, bloody 'ell!" Kate trotted out her British accent. "When did you find this nugget of information?"

"Last night. I couldn't wait to spring it on you. I started to text you, but I wanted to see your face. Imagine—a U.S. Marshal chases you across five states.

Now you're in the same damn little town. Come on Kate, it *is* funny—better yet—it's great publicity."

Susie squeezed Kate's arm. "I'm sorry, you're really upset. Start from what happened today. I'm glad to help, but I don't understand small town shit. I'm a big city girl you know. Why do you care who hears us?"

The waitress appeared with cheese tots. "Can I bring you ladies another round of drinks? Them boys in the corner booth wanna buy you girls a round."

"We would be pleased to accept a drink from those kind gentlemen." Susie attempted a southern belle accent.

"Promise me, Susie, you won't tell anything to anyone. Everyone knows everyone. Everybody is related. I don't know what the hell is going on, so let's keep it to ourselves."

Susie looked around the room. "Them boys are watching us, Kate." She crunched on a cheese bite. "I don't see anything odd. I think you're still paranoid."

Kate ignored Susie's remarks, hoping to tell this part of the story before Susie started a party. "Pops lost the house, maybe everything else. The new owner destroyed the beautiful porch. I don't know why. Why would someone redesign the porch?"

"The porch, really? I thought spouses had rights, is this legal?" Susie asked.

"I don't know, but we're gonna find out. Pops remarried in 1989 so that makes twenty-five years." Kate looked up as she did the addition in her head. "He served as full-time caretaker for the last five years. I guess they thought he would die first, six years her senior and having heart problems."

"More research, my friend, starting with a good lawyer," Kate added.

"Okay, first on my list: research an attorney who specializes in estate planning," Susie volunteered.

"Sounds right, thanks, Susie. I feel like someone hit me in the head. I can't think. You know the history, my grandmother died about a year after my parents were killed in the plane crash. Pops married Grandma Helen three months later. He needed help with me—she found and hired it. I was five, I think."

"Go on."

"Grandma Helen and her first husband owned several pharmacies in the area. Pops was a natural salesman and went to work for the corporation. Grandma Helen's first husband died, and the manager of the stores took advantage of the situation and starting stealing. When she found out, she grabbed her purse, closed all the stores and drove away in her Cadillac. Grandpa Ted helped liquidate her assets. In other words—he saved her ass."

"Your Grandma Helen was a tough ol' gal."

"He told me today he has boxes of records and furniture in storage. It sounded like he has enough furniture for a small apartment and thirty boxes of documents. It's complicated."

"I am so on it, it pays well, right?" Susie sipped her frozen cocktail and glanced around the room. Her eyes stopped at the pool table where the cowboys gathered.

Kate ignored Susie's question and her preoccupation with the cowboys. "I thought they combined their assets. It was none of my business. Pops said he doesn't know how it happened. I don't know—maybe he's acting—or he's starting to get dementia."

"Damn." Susie nodded and slurped her drink. "Or maybe they are drugging him."

"Look who's paranoid now—but that's why I wanted him outta that damn nursing home. It is a substandard facility. Okay, this is where it gets a little *Twilight Zone*. They built the house and then they bought a farm together. She also owned four other farms. You remember the fishing cabin and the long weekend we had not long after we first started working in the bond office?"

"Oh my gosh, we had so much fun. Other than the snakes, the freakin' owl and the mosquitoes, but what a great party! We danced all night."

"Anyway, that property and the cabin on the lake, I thought they owned together. Not so, according to the paperwork. Everything is titled in the Helen Freking Trust. Pops is not the heir—or what they call the trustee."

"Who is?"

"H.O.G.G., some company in town, is the trustee."

"H-O-G-G, hog? How corny is that?" Susie burst out laughing. "How's that even possible?" Heads turned and gawked at the women.

Kate put her finger to her lips and glanced around the room before she continued her story. "Here's the kicker! I'm to inherit the cabin, the lake, the timber and about two hundred acres of land."

"You?" Susie screamed and laughed.

Heads turned again. Kate laughed and felt herself shaking. She realized the alcohol was kicking in and she continued to laugh. "I know, right?"

"Did she even like you? Get out of here! It must be worth a small fortune."

The waitress walked over and cleared the table, "Ya'll want something else?"

"Two burgers, with everything, two side salads—thanks." Kate smiled at the young waitress then followed her gaze to the cowboys playing pool. "I'd like to buy the pool players a round of beer—unless there's a problem?"

"No problem by me," the waitress answered. "The skinny one, he's my baby brother. We like his girlfriend—so don't mess with him, not that you would. The cute one, he's married. Nice, but very married. Miss Sally says to stop by before you leave."

"We're eating burgers? We never eat burgers. You're ordering for me? And who's Miss Sally?"

"We're gonna be glad we ate. Best burgers in town. I feel a party coming on. Let me finish this part—anyway they sold their home and most of the contents at auction, with thirty days to vacate. She dies before the closing. Remember, the house is in her trust. The trustee takes over—seizes all the money. The farm's also seized, credit cards cancelled. Pops has been served papers by the sheriff. Not only has he watched his wife die, lost his house, lost a fortune, they are suing him too. They call it a 'Declarative Judgment.' All those years sitting in court, I've never seen one, have you?"

"No, but that's next on my list. I'll research it. Wow, Kate, you have me captivated. It makes a great story, it would make a great book."

"It's a mess. I can't believe Pops hid this from me just five weeks ago at Grandma's funeral. He made excuses why I shouldn't stay in town. Here he was, Susie, living in a near vacant house. The family dinner was held by the church. I didn't go to the house. He said he wanted me to get my life back. I checked flights and he insisted I go. He seemed fine then. I felt like I deserved a break— I should have stayed. I'm just rambling now. Oh, how he wound up in the nursing home. The trustee for H.O.G.G. evicted him and arranged a room at Squaw Valley."

"Bloody hell, the people who bought the house must be sweating it now."

"I don't think so. Why would you say that?" Kate asked.

"Kate, the owner dies and they know your grandfather built the house and lived in it for twenty-five years. They see the paperwork—your grandfather's name not on the documents—and you don't think they smell anything fishy?"

"Will you stay and help me get to the bottom of it? The five properties and the house are probably worth about two million dollars. Susie, that's it! They gave me the cabin so Pops and I wouldn't sue. That's the piece of the puzzle I've struggled with all day."

"You're paranoid."

"I know, but it does make for a great story." Kate flashed her saleswoman smile. If you stay, it won't be all work, I promise. In fact, I need you to introduce yourself to those cowboys. They were working at the house today. The one in the red shirt is foreman of the crew at Pop's house. He tried to help me today. I think he said his name is Clayton Clark."

"Clayton Clark, Kate, of course you know him. We all danced on the picnic tables out at the cabin. How could you forget?"

Kate stared at the man across the room. "It feels like five lifetimes ago, five states, eight different personas. I'm a different person. I put all of my old life behind me."

"The life you need to leave behind is the one where you had to crawl into the dog house with a pit bull to hide from Reese Matthews. This is your new adventure."

"You're right, of course," Kate said, letting the alcohol sift in. "I've been hiding for five years, no more hiding!"

Kate stood up and raised her glass and shouted. "You ask me if I know 'Dirty Sally?' I knoowww Dirty Sally and drinks are on me!"

CHAPTER FIVE

THE NEW CHIEF

C hief Reese Matthews reached into the file cabinet and pulled out a small gun safe. He placed his thumb to the security pad. A flashing blue light and a "bing" signaled the box unlocked. He removed the items from the safe: a .357 Lady Smith and Wesson—unregistered—two pictures and a flip phone.

Matthews studied the first photo. It captured Kate's essence. A big gorgeous smile lit up her face and spread into her eyes. Her hair was pulled back through a ball cap. She wore cargo pants, a red shirt, and military style boots. The shirt fit in all the right places.

The Chief's face softened as he relaxed, remembering their first conversation. "Don't I know you?" Matthews had tried the lame pickup line.

Kate had laughed at him, extended her hand and shaken his. "I'm Kate Anderson, Court Investigator, your trainer for today. If that was some attempt at flirting—I'm also your employee. I'm the one who works out of your office. My pay comes out of your budget, but the judge makes it clear, I work for him. Your predecessor thought I was a nightmare. You really didn't know me?"

Worst nightmare—an understatement, she remembered. That was six years ago.

"I suppose you think you look like Keanu Reeves," she had said, sipping her Margarita later that night at an eccentric bar on the outskirts of town.

Matthews tore himself away from the picture and picked up the next. This picture, a digitally enhanced blow-up, had been taken at the gravesite of Kate's good friend, Ron Davis. She held a spider-webbed umbrella, dressed in all black clothing, short dress, and tall buckled boots. Her necklace, made of lace, hung down her neck and crept into her cleavage.

I'm missing something.

He studied the picture. She was dressed in Goth: her pale, powdered face, eyebrows arched, lips drawn with black liner, grey lipstick and large black-framed glasses covering her cheek bones. Her oval face was somehow squared.

How can this woman be Kate Anderson? Hiding in plain sight, she deliberately called attention to herself. Matthews pulled out the old flip phone and pressed buttons until he reached the messages. He played the message with Kate's voice.

"Stop chasing me! I don't need saving, Reese." An engine in the background almost drowned out her voice.

He knows now that she climbed in a small plane and took off in a farmer's field. A physical ache spread through Reese's body, an ache he cannot explain. The counselor called it an addiction. *I'm not obsessed with her, I just need to know how she stayed one step ahead of us. I wonder where she is now.*

The intercom interrupted the Chief's thoughts, "Sir, I need to speak to you—immediately."

"Come down, Blakely."

"Damn it. Damn it," Matthews said to the surrounding air. He tossed the pictures and phone into the box and locked it. He stood up and stashed it into the drawer, then crossed the room and opened the door. The pistol—left out on the desk—stayed there. Both men noticed it—like an elephant in the room—but neither brought the subject up.

Steve Blakely, Matthews' assistant at the U.S. Attorney's office, followed Reese Matthews in his career path as small-town police chief. Blakely accepted the assignment of assistant chief. When the team failed to apprehend the fugitive Kate Anderson, both of their careers at the Marshal's office hit a dead end. Blakely took the first job offered to him.

"Sir, I have a full report for you. First off, Kate Anderson is in town. I have the make and model of her car and her location. Her friend, Susie Jones, is also here. All info in this report sir, no picture yet." Blakely tapped the file with his finger and continued. "I believe she will be staying on, sir, her grandfather has gotten himself into some trouble."

"Blakely, you have been invaluable. I hope you will be happy here, and when you have learned all there is to know from me, you should move on and up. I will help you—you know that."

"Yes, sir, I'm banking on it."

"You're one of only a few people who have the balls and courage to be honest with me. It's what I value the most. Do you have any reservations about checking on Kate Anderson?"

"Sir, I'm sure you have your reasons."

If Blakely had concerns about checking up on a private citizen caught up in a murder investigation who had been exonerated, he kept it to himself. A job was a job, and he knew his boss had ties with law enforcement organizations all over the United States. *Just a temporary setback,* Blakely told himself.

"Then continue, Blakely."

"Sir, H.O.G.G., an accounting firm here, is suing Mr. Anderson for the proceeds from his house. Another lawsuit, I think it is a lawsuit, is a competency hearing."

"That's not good. Go on."

"Boss, Mr. Anderson has also been served a subpoena to testify against his brother-in-law."

"How old is he? Where is he now?"

Blakely referred to the file, "Sir, Mr. Anderson is ninety-two, he drives a white, Chevy Malibu, license plate…"

"Never mind that, Blakely. This hog outfit, they plan to drag him into court after how much he has done for this damn town?"

"Sir, and again, I don't have all the facts, but Mr. Anderson resided at the Squaw Valley Nursing Home until yesterday. Kate Anderson rolled into town, checked him out and moved him to the Grand River Bed and Breakfast. Surely, she will move him somewhere more permanent."

Matthews scowled at Blakely. "Go ahead, I know you have saved the best for last."

"On my way back from the courthouse, I heard on the scanner the sheriff's office placed an order to stop and detain a vehicle and driver in connection with 'shots fired' call at a lake house cabin in this county. The vehicle and driver match the description of Miss Anderson."

"Go…get…my car, Blakely."

CHAPTER SIX

GIRLS RUN, BOYS CHASE

K ate sped down the gravel road. A two-ton hay truck loomed large in her rearview mirror. She glanced both ways, blew the stop sign at the blacktop, swerved left and increased her speed. She berated herself for beginning the game. *Girls run, boys chase. I should know that by now.*

After three steep hills, she cut sharp and tore into the next driveway. She pulled around to the side yard, searching for an occupant of the house. With no one in sight, she crept further around the house, tucked away from the road. She parked the SUV heading out. *Those farmhands have been following me since I passed Uncle Bob's barn. I've spent my whole life playing hide and seek. They won't find me until I'm ready.*

As the truck sped by the farmhouse, Kate drove out the other side of the U-shaped driveway. *If they are Uncle Bob's farmhands, they know I will double back to the cabin.*

That should give me a couple of minutes. She pushed the button on the car phone and called Susie. When Susie answered, Kate spoke in a rush. "Listen, can you take Pops to breakfast this morning? Use your charm and pump him for information. Also, listen, a couple more things, quick..."

"Yes, mum!"

"No girl, not like that, I'm not being bossy. I need help," Kate said in a rush.

"What's happening?" Susie said.

"I'm glad I bought the revolver last night, I'll call you in a few."

Kate shot back down the black top, turned right on the gravel road. She made a wide turn, swinging the rear of her vehicle against a gate. She picked up the revolver, stepped out of her vehicle and stood near the wheel. Then she zipped up her black jacket, pulled her hair into her hat and lowered the brim. *Avoid photos — everybody has a cell phone with a camera.*

As the truck slowed and moved towards her, Kate talked to herself. *Wait, wait.* When she could see faces, Kate raised her weapon and fired a shot at the gravel in front of the truck. Boom! The bullet sent rocks flying. The sound echoed through the timber.

The truck slid to a stop in the middle of the gravel road. Kate stood her ground, pistol in hand, arms extended in a straight line. Her heart raced as seconds ticked by. An older man held a phone to his ear; the other two stared. Time seemed to stand still. Finally, the large truck backed down the road and then swung out towards town.

"Don't chase me—assholes!" Kate yelled after them. She pushed the button on her phone. Susie answered immediately. "Hey girl, still in crisis, but would you check east of Kingseat for a town which might have a new rental car?"

"Consider it done."

Kate gazed at her new property. "No Trespassing" signs hung on the locked gate. She stepped up on the first bar and peered over. Beautiful tall oak trees lined the drive and circled the ten-acre lake. She climbed onto the second rung. From there, she could view the timber and crops. A flock of geese circled and landed in formation on the lake, honking at Kate the Intruder. Something about the call of the geese reverberated deep into Kate's soul like a tuning fork and a piano. The words "*called home*" echoed in her brain and spread into the rest of her being. She took a deep breath and marveled at the peaceful setting.

I better go. Kate fought the urge to climb over the gate and check the property. She stepped back into the vehicle, picked up her binoculars and searched the area for the truck. *Did you circle back around, you little sissies?* Satisfied of a clear path, she drove north toward Macon County, then pushed the car phone button to the last phone dialed.

"You scared me, are you all right?"

"Yes, Susie, I'm fine. I will be better when I am out of the county. Did you find me a rental car?"

"Yes, Mum, you will have to drive a little further down the road. There aren't many rental car places in the 'middle of nowhere.' I ordered a new vehicle. I better not ask what you have been up to. We will speak of it later," Susie mocked in her British accent. "I'll text you the address, and I hope you like your new ride.

"Did you know, brandishing a weapon in a rude and menacing manner is a felony in Missouri." Kate studied the road as she talked.

"I did, Katie dear, but I'm glad you went prepared for trouble."

"Be prepared, Girl Scout motto," Kate laughed. "Quick story: some farmhands chased me, and I took a potshot at them. I'm crossing the Macon County line, out of our sheriff's jurisdiction. I doubt the Macon County sheriff cares about a little scuffle in Livingston County. Of course, there's always the highway patrol."

"I'm glad you are very familiar with your law enforcement," Susie said.

"The mongrels will report it to the sheriff's office; Uncle Bob probably has a cop in his pocket. But cops would look for this vehicle coming back into town."

"You're right," said Susie, and added, "I'll text you the address of a car dealership which also has car rentals. I've done some digging into the numerous times your grandmother updated her trust. The first document was thirty years ago and left all six hundred acres to your Uncle Bob. That's her brother, is that correct?"

"Yes, she's my step-grandmother, so technically, he's my step-uncle or is it step-grand-uncle. Something like that."

"I'm going to have to do a flow chart to keep up. Whoever he is, he owns about 1700 acres. Looks like he was empire building and I imagine he is very upset about not inheriting your land."

"How old is the previous document?"

"There were several documents in between, but she did not change it dramatically until a year ago. Your grandparents were frequent visitors at the attorney and the accountant offices. It also looks like your Uncle Bob got a little screwed."

"Wow, farmers and their land, it is always about the land. I'm glad I backed the farmhands off, but it might be a good idea to stay away from here for a while. Let them get used to the idea. I'm sure Bob blames Pops."

"It's probably Pop's fault," Susie said. "But, he did marry her after all. He should be old enough to take care of himself. Does Bob have heirs?"

"No biological children, but I think he raised a nephew. I'm not sure, I never paid any attention. I just avoided him. It's a great piece of property. I'd better concentrate on the roads. Thanks Susie, I'll be back as soon as I can."

"Ta, ta for now." Susie said.

Kate chuckled as she sped further into Grundy County. She turned off her cell phone, avoiding the battery drain that searching for a tower would cause. She would not turn it back on until she arrived in

Macon, Missouri, sixty miles east of Kingseat. She made a large loop skirting two counties, attempting to distance herself from the cabin and any incidents which may have happened there. As she drove from one black top road to the next, she saw small Amish farm houses with large barns and buggies. Clothes danced in the wind, hung on ropes strung post to tree. She traveled for twenty miles before she saw a vehicle other than an Amish buggy.

∾ ∾ ∾

Kate pulled into Woody's Car Dealership on Main Street, Macon, Missouri. A young, handsome car salesman opened the door to the dealership with a grand gesture. His blue blazer stuck on the door handle, but he managed to recover. "How may I help you today, m'lady?"

Geez, English accents everywhere or is he a "Princess Bride" geek. I'm not in the mood for Prince Charming. "Do you have a rental car exchange here?"

"Yes, right over here."

"I should have a car reserved under the name Kate Anderson.

"You're bringing in your SUV and taking a Ford 150 pickup, is that correct?"

Kate laughed. "Sure, why not?"

"Is there a problem?"

44

"I had a sports car in mind. But never mind—what color is the truck?"

"Sky blue, do you want to change your rental? I'm sure we can exchange it, trucks are in high demand in this area."

"Let's go have a look." Kate said.

Kate and the salesman walked out to a large 4-wheel drive pickup. She circled the vehicle and laughed. "I assume this has the push button 4-wheel drive."

"Yes ma'am."

While outside, Kate studied the young man for a minute. She thought he was in his early twenties and finally reached his full height of about 6'3", with blue eyes and a quick smile. "Would you be interested in a little side business? I'll need another vehicle in a few days. A sports car, preferably vintage. I pay cash. I will also need a 30-day registration tag, something not traceable to me."

The young salesman stared at Kate. "Well, let me think," he stammered.

"I need to get a few things out of the SUV while you think about it."

Kate returned and exchanged keys with the salesman. She had operated on the underground economy for the last five years and felt certain she could spot the individuals who took advantage of cash. She gave the him her phone number. "Can you delay the paperwork on this rental car, maybe until late this afternoon?"

"Sure, but It will have to be turned in today." The salesman grinned at her and the two shook hands. "I'll call you in a few days."

"I hope we will do business again soon," Kate said and climbed into the pickup.

ᨏ   ᨏ   ᨏ

Kate synced her phone with the truck and called Susie.

When Susie answered, Kate sang, "You are my sunshine, my only sunshine."

Susie laughed and then reported. "A lovely breakfast was had with your grandfather, Katie dear. Why do you have such trouble with him? I expect you to sort it out."

"Yes, Ma'am," Kate replied in her best southern drawl. "Your Brit speak is perfect as always. Thanks for the truck! It's awesome."

"When you said you were going to 'stay away' from the cabin, I knew you didn't mean it. The truck will give you a few days to explore rural country roads."

"It's perfect Susie, thanks!"

"Kate, here's what Pops told me. He said he thought your Grandmother left him everything in her will. The only stipulation was Bob could farm the properties until his death. Your Uncle Bob is very ill. There were a few instructions for cash gifts to her sorority sisters and for the cemeteries. He has never heard of the other charities.

"Did he say anything about his financial status?"

"No, girl—I grilled him pretty hard, but did not get into his finances. Kate, the last thing he wants is for you to stop your life and take care of him. He is a proud man."

Kate drove back to Kingseat deep in thought. *Pops, what have you gotten us into?*

CHAPTER SEVEN

MEETING WITH THE ACCOUNTANT

The white-haired old man struggled with the car door but exited the vehicle without help. He read the curb before he stepped up, withered hands reaching high in the air. He looked like he was attempting to jump a skateboard up on the curb. Once up, he straightened himself and stood as tall as he could manage. He approached the front of the bank building, walking as if he were still pushing his wife's wheel chair.

Kate watched her grandfather from the car window and then hurried to catch up. She could not get over how much he had aged in the past two months.

The bank had transformed over the years from a small, brick building into a modern, marble structure with twenty-foot glass doors and two-foot-long gold-colored handles. The massive building stood out like an albatross in the historic district. Across the street sat the historic courthouse.

"This way, Katrina, this way." The old man wrestled with the massive door, and with Kate's help, they swung it open. Kate looked around in amazement at the modern new decor in the bank. Pops hurried to the elevator and waved to Kate.

"OK, Pops, I'm coming."

The elevator doors slid open, and they stepped in. Pops pushed the "2" button on the panel and the lift groaned as it rose. Classical music played in the background. Kate checked for cameras and the two rode in silence to the second floor where there were office rentals.

As the door opened, Kate saw the accounting firm's sign to the left and the attorney's sign to the right.

Once inside the attorney's office, Pops walked to the window and said, "Marcie, we're here to see Howard."

"Yes, he is expecting you. We knew you would come early. Follow me, Theodore."

The middle-aged, portly woman ignored Kate and led the way down a short hallway to a conference room. The furniture was dated, but expensive. Law books lined up in the bookshelves, untouched for years, but dusted weekly.

"May I get you coffee or a bottle of water?"

"No, thank you." Kate and Theodore answered in unison and shook their heads.

After an appropriate amount of waiting time, a tall, distinguished man wearing a tailored dark blue suit entered the room.

"Hello, Howard," Kate stood up and shook his hand. Kate's firm handshake was met with a limp rag.

"Hello, Katrina, what can we do for you today?"

"I thought you were retired, Howard," Kate jabbed.

"I work half days, I'm not ready to go out to pasture."

Another man joined them. "This is the trustee of Helen Freking's estate, Anthony Asmus. He is an accountant with the firm next door." Goose bumps crawled up Kate's arm. She did not attempt to shake his hand. Her heart quickened, and she scooted her chair closer to her grandfather.

"The ball's in your court, Katrina," Howard said.

Kate tried to calm her beating heart and was unable to take her eyes off Anthony. She managed to glance at Howard and say, "Her name was Helen Anderson—not Freking. She took the name voluntarily when she married my grandfather twenty-five years ago."

"She chose the name for her trust, it doesn't matter," the attorney explained.

"It matters to us."

"You have no say." Howard said curtly.

"Maybe not, we'll see." Kate moved to Agenda Item # 2. "Grandfather is moving to an apartment."

"He is free to do that," said Anthony.

"Will you arrange for a refund from the nursing home?"

Howard glanced at the accountant. "I don't believe you will have any trouble, but if you do, contact the office and leave a message with Jennifer."

"Howard, weren't you speaking with the director yesterday? He refused to refund the money. You are his attorney, aren't you? Make the call, save us all some trouble." Katrina didn't wait for him to speak. "It is my understanding the trustee plans to seek guardianship of my grandfather in court."

"Your grandfather says he does not remember his wife signing papers to donate her farms to charity. He attended every meeting, and we have documentation. We had no choice but to file for a competency hearing," Howard said.

"Drop the case." Kate glanced at her grandfather. His jaw was set in a hard line, his white face flushed red. "I also understand the trustee plans to retain the money from the sale of my grandfather's house."

"That is correct," the attorney said.

"How can you do that?"

The attorney sighed and stated, "The house was listed in the Helen Freking Trust. The house sold at auction. She died four days before the closing. It is a trust asset. No questions, no arguments. Your grandfather signed his rights away in 1993."

Kate looked directly at the accountant. "The day after my grandmother died, why did you tell my grandfather he would receive the money from the house?"

Anthony lunged across the table at Kate. "I'm the Trustee, that's why."

Kate's heart lurched, but she did not flinch. Years of interviewing criminals in jails prepared her for this meeting. She waved her hand in front of her nose hoping to signal to the trustee he had bad breath.

He glared at Kate, "You little twit."

51

"Now we have it. You took the bait, Anthony. You can glare at me and get in my face, but you don't scare me. You did not answer my question." Kate's voice rose, and she accented every word. "Why did you tell Theodore he would receive the money from the house?"

The attorney stepped in. "Anthony is not an attorney. He did not write the trust and it was not his call. Yes, it's true, if she had lived, your grandparents could have done whatever they wanted with the money, but that's not what happened. We intend to manage the money according to Helen's wishes, donating to the six charities specified. The only way you can break this trust is to prove she was incompetent at the time she signed the last revision of the trust."

"Or Howard, maybe *you* were incompetent." Kate shot back.

"Me? Damn it—you wouldn't dare!"

"Yes, I will dare." Kate sat up tall and leaned across the table closer to the attorney's face. "Every revision since 1993 gave my grandfather the right to stay in the house until his death. Why was the house left out of this last revision?"

"Of course, it was left out!" the attorney shouted. "Your grandparents were selling it. There was no need to mention it. No one thought she was going to die."

"*Everyone* thought she was going to die!" Kate shouted back at the flushed attorney. "She broke her back, she broke her hip. She refused treatment for the large mass growing in her stomach. She was in hospice. I was fifteen hundred miles away, and I knew she was dying."

"Bullshit!" the attorney roared.

The accountant stepped in and slid a stack of papers over to Kate. "Here's the information regarding your inheritance. We now need some information from you."

Kate noticed her grandfather fidgeting in his pocket.

"How many farms were there?" the accountant asked.

"Five or six—about 600 acres," Kate said, watching her grandfather's hands under the table.

"Describe them," the accountant demanded.

"No, thank you. Pops, let's go. The attorney should have all the information regarding the farms."

Pops stood up with ease and poked Kate, showing her a set of brass knuckles, his hand barely hidden under the table. She smiled, patted him on the back. "Let's go, Pops." She led them out of the room.

The attorney shouted at the two as they left the room. "You file to have the trust broken and you will lose your farm!"

Kate and Theodore ignored him and retraced their steps to the elevator. "Let me see those brass knuckles. Pops, you crack me up!" Kate laughed. "Those are illegal."

"Katrina, I'm too old to care."

When the two arrived back at the car, Kate slid in the driver's seat and watched her grandfather reach up for the hand hold and then slowly fold himself into the seat.

"We need to find a different attorney," Kate said.

Pops started coughing, his frail body heaving with the struggle to breathe. "She left me nothing."

"Are you all right? Do you need to see a doctor?"

The old man's body wracked with a coughing fit. "No, no—just take me back to the B&B, it's just my heart cough, I'll be all right."

"How about a sip of water?" Kate handed Pops a bottled water.

"How about a whiskey?"

"It wouldn't be the first time we were drinking before noon."

"Medicinal purposes," Pops said between coughing and sips of water.

Kate, alarmed, studied her grandfather's face before starting the car.

"Pops, do you have a heart pill or a flask?"

He ignored her and said, "Your Grandma Helen thought the world of Anthony. We both trusted him. She gave him credit for helping save her business. They took us out for my birthday dinner. They were just pretending to be our friends. I wanted to leave you some money when I died. I'm a stupid old fool."

"Pops, I have money. You invested in my life insurance and monitored my trust. I just inherited a farm from Grandma Helen. Her money was also your money, you were husband and wife for twenty-six years. Let's concentrate on fishing and making plans for the cabin. When's the last time you went fishing?"

The old man did not respond. His cough subsided. A dark cloud seemed to cover their little white car as they drove home. Kate was also defeated. There was nothing she could say to make him feel any better.

"Right now, let's go get a bite to eat."

"No, no. I'm not hungry. Katrina, take me back to the B&B, I'm very tired."

"Pops, I don't know why Grandma Helen liked him, he reminded me of a serial killer."

"Sounds about right," Pops said.

CHAPTER EIGHT

DOCTOR, DOCTOR

D r. Terrance Williams found himself reminiscing about his thirty years of work in Kingseat. His private office contained a large oak desk, bookshelves lined with medical books, signed wildlife original prints and framed collections of feathers, arrow-heads and duck calls. A patron of the local arts and various charities, he'd bought the items at charity auctions. The displays served as conversation pieces and impressed the patients and businessmen who visited him, but Williams had no attachment to them. They were just props for the part he played as the local doctor.

His mind lingered on the day he met one of the members of the secret society dubbed "The Founders." While still in med school, a wealthy real estate developer visited him on campus and explained how the meetings worked and how he could retire a very rich man. Kingseat needed a doctor, and he met their criteria: male, white, ambitious.

Dr. Williams tore himself away from his memories and called for his nurse. *I hope Cammie wore her nurse's uniform with the short skirt today.*

She did not disappoint. "Good morning, Doctor. You're in early this morning."

"You look lovely, Cammie, you're wearing my favorite skirt."

"Thank you, Doctor. Can I get you coffee? I just added a little nutmeg, the way you like it." Cammie walked around the desk and ran her perfectly polished nails up his back.

"No, thank you, I grabbed a cup at home. I'm just checking the roster for morning rounds at the nursing home."

"I diverted all your patients to the nurse practitioner this morning. Let's run out to your country house. I'll pack a lunch." Cammie leaned over the doctor's desk— he viewed her bright red bra with a tiny pink bow, barely covering ample cleavage. He sat back in his chair. She hiked up her skirt to straddle him, but he moved away.

Cammie and the doctor started their three-year affair the minute she walked in the door as his temp nurse. He had not settled on Cammie as his permanent companion. *Tomorrow afternoon, after depositing my money from The Founders, I will be a multi-millionaire. And, when I sell the building, this crappy art collection, the cars, my houses... why should I settle?*

"Not now, Cammie—sorry. Why don't we get all our work caught up and we can have a weekend in the city?

I have some preparation for the meeting tonight—you arrange for a nice hotel room and I'll provide the plane. You would like a little plane ride, wouldn't you, sweetie?"

Cammie smiled and turned, "Maybe I'm busy this weekend." She walked away from him.

"Come back here, you little tease, don't you dare be busy this weekend." *I smell a hint of desperation. Oh, it's her biological clock.*

She started her walk back, looked him straight in the eye, and slid her skirt up. Exposing a hint of lace, she paused and lifted her skirt higher, then turned and left the room.

The doctor stood up and looked at the back door. No distractions today. *When my business is done, I will just fly away—single and free.*

৵ ৵ ৵

Once at the nursing home, Doctor Williams strolled through the hallway with a swagger of authority. He looked at all the nurses and ranked them according to his checklist. A bad cliché, but ten ranked best in his mind. Dr. Williams grew up on hand-me-down Playboys from the 60's. He loved big breasts. He also loved long legs, small waists and tight asses. Other points on his list included sexiness, kindness, intelligence, ability to cook and willingness to serve, not necessarily in that order.

Should I check on Theodore? Probably not, I've grown fond of the old man. It will be hard to see him go. But go, he must. The doctor smiled to himself.

Theodore had served his purpose—The Founders confiscated four hundred acres of farm land and most of his wife's money. The meeting tonight would decide who would get the chance to buy one of the farms cheap—and flip it for a huge profit. The doctor pulled out the prescription pad from his pocket, clicked his pen and scribbled "Trazadone, 50 mgs. at night." He scribbled another prescription for "Xanax, .5 mgs. four times per day."

The director of the nursing home had assigned Theodore to the last room. "Last" means last: last fed, last bathed, and last checked on. By the time the nurses wrestled all the other patients to the dining room, if the old man were still awake, they would feed him. If not, they would let Theodore sleep. It would not take long for him to become too weak, tired and groggy to care.

The doctor stopped to talk to Harriett. *She is perfect. If my wife had not been such a bitch during the divorce proceedings, I'd be with her right now instead of the crazy Cammie Martin.*

"Good morning Doctor," Harriett said. "I just wanted to say congratulations on the plaque you received at the football award ceremony the other night. You have donated thousands of hours of service."

Too bad she married that farmer. "Thank you, Harriet. You are very kind."

59

"We're going to miss you around here, but congratulations on your retirement. Do you mind my asking if you have plans?"

"Lots of plans, Harriett—maybe we could get a drink some night and I will tell you about them." *I bet she's a spitfire in bed.*

"Doctor, you are so funny—you know I can't do that—I'm married."

"Yes, Harriett, I'm teasing. I'm taking a few people from the hospital on plane rides, after I retire, of course. Consider it a little going-away present from me. It might be my first hobby after retirement. I think you deserve a little reward for all your work. Do you think your husband would let you go for a plane ride with me? You know, I'm harmless."

Harriett smiled, "Thank you, yes, I will ask Michael about it. I know— he could come too."

Not exactly what I had in mind. "Let's get back to the matter at hand, shall we? First on the list—Theodore Anderson, how is Mr. Anderson today?"

"He's been discharged."

"What?" the doctor asked.

Harriett moved away from the doctor. "I'm sorry, doctor— we notified your office yesterday."

He wadded up the two prescriptions, threw them in the trash can, and stormed off.

CHAPTER NINE

RECRUITMENT OF DON

T ypical of many small midwestern towns, Kingseat, Missouri had a coffee shop in the square across from the courthouse. Mug Shot Cafe filled up each morning with people attending court for speeding tickets, criminal charges, and divorces.

The Liar's Table was where the local crowd sat for a quick breakfast before work. Customers rotated there all morning: a plumber, a farmer, an old guy who sat for two hours and left a quarter tip.

The developer, most just called him "Tucker," attended "real regular." His big fancy house sat at the edge of town. His wife held bridge clubs and sorority meetings. Today, dressed like a simple farmer, he made his morning rounds, visiting the coffee shop and talking about the weather, crops in the field, and hunting season. The topic eventually turned to the morning's gossip. The developer's ears pricked up when it came to who died—and who was in the hospital. Tucker took pride in his reputation. The coffee clubbers called him "The Vulture" and he thrived on the title.

A local attorney, Donald Armstrong, walked into the café and swung his briefcase into the front booth of the restaurant. The talk stopped at the Liar's Table as they turned to look at the attorney sitting in the front booth by the large dirty windows.

Tucker got up and sauntered over to join the attorney. He leaned over, and in hushed tones whispered, "We need you to take over the Helen Freking Trust case."

"You're outta your friggin' mind!" the attorney shouted at his unwelcome visitor.

"This is the last thing *The Founders* will ask of you. I understand your hesitation. You like the girl, it's sweet," the developer said. "But, the consensus remains, you are the best man for the job. The girl respects you.

"She's not a girl. Kate Anderson is a woman with a history of outmaneuvering morons like you. You need to do your homework," Don said.

"She might even listen to you." The developer continued his speech without any acknowledgement of Don's outburst. "The attorneys say you two had a fling, when she worked as a court investigator."

Don's faced turned red. "We did not have a fling. She's smart and has an investigative mind. She's capable of breaking your little secret society wide open. If anything, Kate and I remain adversaries."

"All the better," Tucker said.

"Just pay her off, let the old man have his money. I understand you want those farms, they are in the grand scheme of *The Founders'* plan. Take the farms, but let him have his house-money and dignity."

"We've already decided, we voted last night." The developer took a toothpick from behind his ear and started picking his teeth, settling on one molar on the bottom right corner of his mouth. He might be worth millions, but without his wife in the room, he had the manners of a barbarian.

"Let me tell you a story about this girl. I was new in town, just been appointed by the governor to fill the vacant prosecuting attorney spot. Some idiot kid decided to make obscene phone calls to Kate—vulgar, nasty phone calls in the middle of the night, stalking her, window peeking. She might have been seventeen at the time. He was in high school. I warned the kid's parents—I won't say their names, but—he had a screw loose, wouldn't stop following her, totally obsessed. That's how I found out about your little secret society: the meetings, the planning of bilking old people out of their money, buying and selling of property and scratching each other's back. The kid's father, a Founder, offered me a piece of the action. I declined. Your whole scheme makes me sick. We owe it to our elders to respect them and take care of them, not rob them."

"I didn't come to get a history lesson—-or ethics for that matter. I came to deliver orders," Tucker said.

"You better shut up and listen. She figured out who it was on her own. He flunked a grade of high school and was a big kid. She knocked on his door, kicked him in the groin, and basically beat the crap out of him."

"So, what's your point, Don?"

"Let me finish. His daddy pressed charges against Kate. Sheriff interrogated her for hours, threw her in a cell. Tough as nails that girl."

"Okay, okay, the girl's got moxie, and I'm bored," Tucker said.

"Her one phone call, while in custody, she didn't call her grandfather. She called Clifford Baxley, attorney at law, who later became the "Iron Fist" judge. I was a new prosecutor running for re-election. You're damn straight, I prosecuted the kid for harassment on three counts. Baxley, a powerful man, sat next to her in court. I kept telling her she didn't need an attorney. At age seventeen, she understood power. She kept me in line. In court, she played the little innocent girl. She looked like she might be thirteen, dressed in a pink polka dot dress, no makeup, her hair worn in a ponytail with a bow. I will never forget how young she looked."

"Yeah, right, so?" The big man stopped picking his teeth, rearranged himself in his chair and stared at the attorney. "Give me more details about the girl."

"Shut up, you pervert. The associate judge threw him the max sentence. It only amounted to ninety days. The pervert got privileges the last twenty days of his incarceration and what did he do? He called her. The jail recorded his calls. Slam dunk case. She left for college, doesn't want to press charges."

"While she was in college, the kid died. End of story. I've often wondered who killed that kid. Was it suspicious? Hell yes, but in this county, it's not murder unless someone cares. No one cared to investigate. The kid was a menace—a budding rapist. I think his own father feared the boy. The sheriff didn't investigate, the coroner called it "natural causes." Twenty-year-old young man dies, no one investigates. Doctor MacMillan, one of your Founders, signed off. That was the first suspicious death tied to that girl."

"Interesting story, Don, I didn't know this. But we voted last night and we want you to proceed. We aren't *asking* you to do this, we're *telling* you to do it. File whatever. You're in charge—put the maximum amount of stress on the old man. Drag his sorry ass into court, embarrass the hell out of him, in the end take his money."

"What about Howard? Why can't he do it?"

"C'mon, you're an attorney. Howard served as a joint attorney for the old man and old lady. He had to recuse himself. If there is a response to the declaratory judgment, Howard could be called as a witness. We need a new lawyer. It's you."

"In other words, you don't have another loser like me," Don said.

"You get the point. Anderson is ninety-two, he's lost his wife, his home, his fortune, and he's got one foot in the grave. The girl doesn't live here. She has a life somewhere else. Besides, we're being very generous—she inherited a farm worth about five hundred thousand. We could have easily taken it all."

Don tried one last feeble attempt. "Think about this, two deaths tied to this girl. Robert O'Dell was the sheriff's cousin. Reese Matthews is a badger, a tracker, he always gets his perp. She had resources to keep one step ahead of him. You are asking for trouble."

"We've got too many years and hours into pulling this off. Twenty-five years of talking those two, elderly people into 'giving away the farm', so to speak. In the end, the attorney had a hell of a time getting that old lady to sign the papers." Tucker leaned in to whisper, "just between you and me, we're a little over-extended on a few of our projects. We need the cash to make some payments. You know how this works, we move money around, but it's time to get some new cash."

Don stared at the man. "You mean your band of merry Robin Hoods transfer funds from one foundation to another?"

The developer slicked his hair back and continued, "Let's just forget I said that. Listen, Don, I don't wanna play this card, but we have kinky pictures of your daughter." He grinned and scooted around in his chair, like a dog rubbing its butt across the carpet.

Don stood up. "I've got court. I don't ever want to see or hear from you again. Not in court, not by telephone. You better watch your back. I will call the trustee today and work through him. Yes, I have a price.

I need to leave this fucking town. All my assets are now for sale and they better sell fast. Get one of your real estate agents over to my office this morning."

The developer rose slowly from the chair. Age crept up on him a little more each day. "Our children are a disappointment, aren't they? One thing we have in common."

Don turned his back and left the restaurant. He knew about the pictures and he didn't want them to ruin his daughter's life. He didn't want to think about it. To his relief, a memory entered his mind and like pushing "play" on a recorder, he thought about Kate's smile and the way she made him feel important.

A blue, four-wheel-drive pickup was parked in the courthouse parking lot. Inside the truck sat a young woman dressed in bib overalls and a John Deere hat. From her parking place she could see the accountant's office, most of who came and went at the courthouse, and several attorney's offices. Long-lens camera in hand, she snapped pictures of the men in the front booth and the ones exiting the diner.

CHAPTER TEN

THE CASE

K ate Anderson swung open the heavy oak door to the courthouse. The wind blew an autumn gale that flung the door into the inside wall of the historic building. She stumbled as she blew into the large entryway.

Mid-center of the wide hallway, the sheriff's deputy watched. Dressed in a brown uniform, black boots, full gear—sidearm, baton, mace and handcuffs—he studied her as she surveyed her surroundings. The deputy waited. Kate took her time. She wore a short, grey wool coat and a cashmere animal print scarf. Her accessories accented her long dark hair. She smiled as she approached the deputy, changing to a more feminine gait as she neared him.

"Good morning." She smiled up at him.

"Good morning, ma'am, attorney?"

"No." *It was the look I was going for—good.*

As she proceeded through the metal detector, the deputy asked, "Do you have business here this morning, ma'am?"

"Yes, Circuit Court."

Kate knew the deputy watched as she stepped on the first marble stair and touched the walnut stair railing. She marveled at the beauty of the wood and took her time caressing it as she climbed the staircase. Light poured through the window and she felt at home, somewhat like when she went to her neighborhood church and lit candles praying for special intentions.

Her memory rewound like a clock turning back the time. Step by step, the months swept back in time. The imaginary clock stopped at a time when she worked this court house. Kate had chosen this assignment because many were afraid of the judge and his strict code of conduct. She knew it would give her a certain status to offset how young she appeared. She had known the judge for years, but they kept the secret to themselves. Those were the days when she wore a red designer suit with black peek-a-boo heels. A woman in a sea of men dressed in black suits and blue ties.

She could see herself, like in a movie, sprinting up the steps. Her title was Investigator for the Circuit Court, a job where she walked a careful tightrope between sheriff, prosecuting attorney and judge. She wrote recommendations for bail and for sentencing according to Missouri guidelines. If Kate recommended no-bail, the offender was out of luck.

Kate knew the court system. She had watched the attorneys in back room deals for years. She suspected corruption in this case, but she did not know what to do about it.

She fought back to the present, noticing how little had changed in the almost six years she had been gone. A "NO SPITTING" sign met her at the second-floor landing. The antique sign from the early 19th century, now framed, brought back more memories.

Money well spent. Kate read about the two-million-dollar restoration of the historic courthouse. "Restoration completed by raising funds in the community and with the generous support of the local trusts and foundations."

She checked her surroundings: office, office, bathroom, courtroom and elevator. *Elevator, what a luxury.*

Kate's pace picked up as she climbed to the third floor. She knew she was early, but it was "game time." She needed to get her head into the present. A little aerobic activity was the best way she could do that. *It smells better.* She sprinted up the last twelve steps to the third floor.

She arrived at the entrance of the courtroom and was surprised to see Buddy, the U.S. Marshal, the ever-faithful sentry at the door. Like the courthouse, he looked the same. Tall, handsome in his navy blue sports coat, white shirt and tie, tan pants.

Kate smiled. "Hello, I'm here for case H.O.G.G. vs. Theodore S. Anderson," she stated before he had time to ask. *His cologne is still Brute.*

Buddy moved aside and with mock gallantry swung the heavy oak door wide open. Just as if it were yesterday, he said, "Good morning, Miss Anderson. Good to see you again."

"Good to see you, Buddy. I wish it were just a visit."

"Do you know the defendant?"

"Yes, he's my grandfather."

Kate walked into the Courtroom and sighed. *I love court.* She thought it was like a dramatic play at the local theatre. Everyone had their places, their roles, their patterns. It was a blood sport. The defendants left crushed and bruised. The spotless, well-groomed lawyers in suits never bled. *Maybe one will today.*

Kate spotted the attorneys all in their places: her grandfather's attorney, the attorney for some of the charities, the attorney for H.O.G.G., trustee of the Helen Freking Trust, Donald Armstrong—a man whom Kate had believed was a friend.

She breathed a sigh of relief when she verified her grandfather was not in court. She noted the trustee did not bother to make an appearance.

So... you can sue someone for $191,000 in Chariton County Circuit Court and not bother to walk across the street and show up for the proceedings. Times have changed.

The bailiff appeared and announced in a single breath, "All rise! The Chariton County Circuit Court is now in session, The Honorable Judge Margaret Chrystal presiding. You may be seated."

As always, the crowd was taken by surprise. Most people struggled to their feet and then were told to be seated. Kate orchestrated the up and down without missing a beat, almost a little curtsy.

She assessed her surroundings. She believed the deputies' focus would be on the judge or the circuit clerk. Buddy's focus would be on the judge's safety. Lawyers and clients would change places on stage. She thought she could slap Don, turn, walk out of the court room, down one flight of stairs and into the women's bathroom. Or, after slapping him, she could go sit down, wait for an arrest and use the thirty-one one hundred dollar bills she had stuffed into her bra for bail money.

Donald Armstrong stood before the judge. Many years ago, he had been her adversary—the target of her practical jokes. Later, as her ally, she laughed at his jokes, and gossiped. She admired him for his refusal to abuse his power and for his ethics. Times had changed. *Why doesn't he offer a compromise? These are charities, for God's sake.*

Armstrong took center stage. Kate thought he looked like Punxsutawney Phil in a cheap J. C. Penney suit. A circus ringmaster performer, he grinned and glad handed all the attorneys, especially her grandfather's. He looked around and saw Kate. *Yes, I'm watching—asshole.*

Then he shook hands with the attorney for the Catholic Church and the Prayer House. Another attorney stepped forward, and then another and another, each representing one of the five charities. Every law firm in town billed for this lawsuit.

"Your Honor, this case is to be set for trial," said Armstrong. The attorneys looked down at their phones and calendars.

"Mr. Armstrong, if you please, can I get introductions this morning?" the judge said.

Armstrong looked a little sheepish, but spoke next, "Donald Armstrong for H.O.G.G."

Each attorney introduced himself and named his client.

The Circuit Clerk handed the judge some dates.

"Yes, your Honor. The case will be settled. H.O.G.G. is dropping the case regarding Mr. Anderson's competency hearing. He has relinquished his rights regarding the proceeds of the sale of the house—$191,000. You see your Honor, the charities voted unanimously: they want the money, your Honor."

Another court date, another round of billing, and all bills wrapped around to Theodore Anderson. Kate watched the attorneys as they nodded and agreed.

"Set your date, Counselor."

Kate blushed in anger. *How could this happen? How could charities vote to participate in a lawsuit to take money from that old man? Do they care if he has enough money to live on?*

She watched as the attorneys switched places. With all these thoughts in her head, she stood up and stepped into the aisle—perfect timing for Armstrong's approach. She blocked his exit.

"Hello, Don."

Before Don could respond, Kate punched him in the face.

CHAPTER ELEVEN

TRESPASSING

K ate climbed the inside stairway of the dilapidated building. She tested the last step and hoisted herself onto the flat roof. She crouched low, letting her eyes focus as she located her partner. He was lying on the opposite side of the roof, binoculars pointed at the downtown square below.

"Get down," a low, hoarse voice said from the other side of the building.

Kate ducked, crossed the distance, and eased down next to Reese. "Wow, you can see the entire downtown square from up here. What's going on?"

"Keep your voice down, I understand the sheriff is looking for trespassers."

Kate dropped her head and placed her hand over her mouth to stifle a laugh. "Hard to miss the 'No Trespassing' signs and the yellow tape strung on the ladder. What is this place anyway?"

"It was an original stagecoach station. Pretty neat building. An old couple ran a bed and breakfast here for years, mostly catering to 'big city' deer and duck hunters."

"The city is tearing the building down," Reese said.

"How did you get up here? That ladder was treacherous. There's no way you hauled your fat ass up here."

"The stairs."

"Oh, funny. My fear of heights, ha, ha, I suppose I deserved that."

Reese showed Kate his iPhone. The video of Kate's derriere climbing the ladder in her skinny jeans appeared on the screen. "Worked out great, didn't it?"

She punched him in the arm and laughed. "Okay, cool, payback prank. Where was the camera, I didn't spot it."

"Camouflaged trail cam. About my waist high. Yep, worked great."

"So—what's going on, anyway?"

"The old attorney went into the bank about an hour ago and he's not come out."

"That's it? An attorney goes into the bank? Sounds like a bad joke. Are you sure he didn't come out on the other side?"

He glared at her. "I live here. I bought a calendar and filled in the blanks. The Elks meeting is always the same. I filled in the Eagles, Masons, churches, City Council meetings and all the county committees, you know, all the local groups. Today is Law Day for the circuit court. Attorneys are in town. It's worth a shot,

Kate, but I don't know if anything is happening. Like I said in my text, it's a stakeout."

Kate rummaged through her bag to find her petite binoculars. She peered at the buildings. "It looks surreal up here in the semi-darkness. Are we lying in rat poop?"

"By the way, I hear there was some excitement in court today."

"Did you get a call from her highness the Honorable Judge Chrystal?" Kate gave Reese the stink eye.

"No, we met at the coffee shop. I hear you gave Don a big, fat, bloody nose."

"I didn't mean to punch him. I meant to slap him. I forgot, I have the right to remain silent, especially with 'yo new title'—Police Chief. No one seemed to notice, I swear, Buddy turned his head and missed the whole thing."

"Oh, they noticed. The sheriff said you almost knocked Don down. You caught him before he went down, straightened his tie, patted him on the shoulder, and strolled out of the courtroom. Cool as a cucumber."

"That is a very vivid picture. I assume—cameras in the courtroom. Do they think I'm going to dye my hair and run? I suppose every deputy and cop watched it." Kate flushed red with embarrassment. "Can we change the subject?"

"Cutting your hair would be fine with me. I like the Meg Ryan look—short and sassy." He grinned. "Here, take some pictures. It will give you something to do and maybe it will keep your mouth shut." He handed her a camera.

They were both silent a moment, lost in their own thoughts.

"Kate, give me your theory." Reese finally broke the silence.

"This isn't the Pelican Brief, I'm not Julia Fucking Roberts."

"Okay, okay, drama queen. Why so grouchy? I know you have some type of theory," Reese said.

"You tell me to shut it, now talk. Men, they think women are bad. Let's just say there is a secret group, society, organization. Maybe it started in the early 80's when the farming bubble burst and many of the local farmers went bankrupt. When the farmers filed bankruptcy, the stores struggled. Taxes stopped flowing in, the roads got bad, more stores closed, and a real depression crisis began."

"Domino effect…it happened," Reese whispered in the darkness. "The farmers lobbied the state and federal governments and they held a 'Farm Aid' concert. Willie Nelson and Rick Springsteen played in a concert north of town. Of course, this happened before your time."

"Way before my time, but I've been researching. It's on YouTube. And I'm grouchy because there may be a warrant out for my arrest for assault."

"There's no warrant. The sheriff and I had a little talk. And, well, nobody saw the assault, and nobody cares. Or everybody saw it, and nobody cares. Don probably thinks he deserved it, or he liked it."

Kate saw his white teeth flash in a familiar grin, "Or you fixed it for me?"

"Well, no, but I'll be glad to take the credit. Don't shoot anybody, okay? I can't help you with that."

"This is what I think happened next. The YMCA, funded by the community and the Budweiser Foundation, raised money and built a center. It was the first sign of life this town had in years. The YMCA brought people to town. Their little darlings played baseball and basketball and soccer. Parents bought gas, shopped in stores, and ate fast food. Tax dollars started to flow in from other counties. As the YMCA grew, the organizers paid attention. Let's say, that group or another group got together and said, 'What we need is more foundations, more trusts, which translated to more old people die and leave their money to the town.' The idea got better and better."

"You *did* have a theory, based on some facts. What if we built a group, a 'secret society' specifically designed to analyze the town's needs and to target old people for their money? Who would we need?" speculated Reese as he picked up his binoculars and looked down at the town.

"At first it would be a small group. We would have to be secret and dedicated to meeting and scheming. First it would be people we could trust, but in the end— bankers, lawyers, accountants, appraisers, city officials, county officials, insurance agents, possibly an auctioneer or some kind jewelry broker. We would have to try to launder the money," Kate said.

Reese turned and grinned at her. "It sounds to me like you've given this some thought, Julia Roberts."

She looked over the back of the buildings and the signs read: jeweler, attorney at law, antiques and collectibles. She snapped some photos. "They wouldn't even need to leave the square."

"Have you researched the local paper to check what trusts are involved?" Reese asked.

"We've scratched the surface. Susie is brilliant, but this was years in the making. And, trusts like my Grandma Helen's—there's no probate, there's no filing with the Secretary of State. Did you know this town has more trusts than most regions? We've been able to track about twenty million in foundation assets in this town of about eight thousand people."

Reese whistled.

"New hospital, refurbished library, a new high school—with a new stadium. Lovely parks, the new swimming pool—it seems the city planners have money for everything. If they can't get the votes for new taxes, somehow the foundations join forces and make it happen. I think it's the Masons."

"It's not the Masons."

"How do you know?"

"I'm a Mason. They don't have any money."

"You're a Mason?"

"Stop looking at me like I turned into an alien. I'm an Elk, an Eagle, a Mason, a member of the NRA, and the rural fire department. It's a small town, people get involved or go crazy. Besides, how do you think I get my political appointments?

"You just got back here, how did you manage all this? Please tell me about the Masons. Are you the Grand Wizard or something?"

"I kept my memberships. I've been here a month and I've been to four meetings. That's the Masonic Temple right over there, and that's all I'm saying about them."

Kate stared at the Masonic Temple and waited, hoping Reese would say more.

"Look! Here comes the accountant."

Reese made a slicing finger across his throat motion, indicating she should shut it.

Kate looked through the binoculars. The accountant turned into a small, dark alley and stopped. "What's he doing? Is that a keypad?"

"I'll be damned, I've walked that alley, never noticed it."

"It looked like he just disappeared. Where the attorney goes, the accountant follows. He's a scary dude, by the way."

"Look, Councilman Tollerton, his day job is the local jeweler."

"When it gets dark, all the cockroaches come out," Kate said.

"Let's say it's true. There is a secret society, a tribunal of men who meet regularly. They target elderly people who have money. The attorneys and accountants advise their clients to put their money into revocable trusts and encourage them to leave some money for charity. Even so, I don't think it's illegal," Reese said.

"I know. I don't know whether I feel better or worse."

"Run away with me."

She looked at him in the semidarkness. "Crap—this again?"

"You really know how to cut the legs out from underneath a guy."

"You know how I feel about you, Reese, but I closed that door a long time ago. You thought it was your duty to save me. You'll try again—you're trying now. I don't need or want saving. I'm a big girl, perfectly capable of making my own decisions."

"I know…can't blame a guy for trying. Stars are coming out."

"Can you go on, now?"

"Leave you here to gaze up at the stars in the rat poop—or plan revenge?"

"No, I just need some time to think. I know my way out."

The chief squatted as he crab-walked across the darkness of the roof. "Will I see you before you leave town?"

"Take your damn camera or I will."

"Don't get caught. I hear the Chief of Police is a hard ass."

CHAPTER TWELVE

THE VLOG

S usie found an apartment on the second floor of a downtown business. It faced Main Street and the recent renovation added a small "Romeo and Juliette" balcony on the second floor. Susie added a small wrought-iron table and chairs for decoration. Kate teased Susie about how odd it would be drinking morning coffee in their pajamas from the little balcony looking onto Main Street with cars rushing past, a stark contrast to their luxury condos overlooking Tampa Bay. They chose the apartment because it turned out to be by far the most modern and the only one with the required two bedrooms and two baths. Susie charmed the owner and paid cash.

Kate lounged sideways across the white cotton slipcovered chair. "Hey Susie, come here."

Susie was setting up the wide screen computer for their next Vlog. "What, love?" Susie responded, dressed in a short lacy pink slip, her hair done up in ribbons and ringlets, her lips painted bright pelican pink—barefoot, her strapped high heels not far away.

"Look at this article in the newspaper. I can't believe it. The city gave an Extraordinary Citizen award to an attorney for stealing money away from elderly people."

"It says that in the paper?" Susie skipped across the room in the apartment. She grabbed the newspaper from Kate and turned to the computer screen as if she were reading to an audience. "This is how you do it Kate, practice, practice. The camera loves me because I play with it." Susie read out loud, bending her abundant cleavage to the camera, and read in a mock British accent, "The Chariton County Community Foundation presented a plaque to long-time member and attorney, Robert Shannon. His efforts led to the receipt of the Ely Smith estate. The estate, amount undisclosed, was donor directed half to the school and the other half to the local hospital."

Susie returned to her new fake southern accent. "You've got to be kidding me! They're rewarding him for pursuing a man's estate?"

"Keep reading."

Susie continued to her mock audience, "In 2014 Shannon was also instrumental in obtaining the Mildred Perkins permanent Endowment Fund which is unrestricted and can be granted to any Chariton County charity. Shannon, the driving force behind these two projects, should be commended as he releases funds after a Board's approval."

Kate grabbed the newspaper back from Susie. "This is the law firm I used to negotiate the lease on the cabin.

Forget it, I'm filing it, I'll deal with it later. Let's talk about the Vlog. It brings in the most cash. You hired some girls to help?"

"It's just a little practice tonight. We're doing the skit you wrote about these young girls taking selfies. We need new blood, new faces. I'm just auditioning them, so you don't need to stay. It's two nursing students from the college and they need some cash."

"It's your baby, but please make them sign all the forms."

"Confidential form, the private contractor agreement, and, of course, the no compete clause. They will come prepared with costumes and add their comments or costumes to the script. I added fifty dollars to your budget for costumes. Seriously, Kate, how were they supposed to get costumes for one hundred dollars?"

"Like I said, this is your production, but in Missouri, they would find a way. How are we doing on cash?"

"Your car purchases ran us a little low, but your Tampa apartment is now booked for the season on Home Away. Unfortunately, that means you are stuck here. This place is cheap, the furniture inexpensive and the utilities are low. I get why people live in the country, except for the lousy weather and nothing at all to do. I emailed you the exact numbers, but we acquired twenty new patrons this month. We are right on track as far as money goes. These new girls will bring us a surge of new sponsors and patrons. I keep finding little editing jobs of my own and you did those two investigative jobs which took you all of five. It would be nice if your book would take off. It might, if you would agree to do some presentations."

"Oh yes, that really brings in the dough. I usually don't break even. Long term, maybe it'll pay off," Kate held her hands up in mock surrender. "The mantra from my writer friends is: the second one sells the first one, so I should leave and put my butt into my writing chair."

Always the actress, Susie rolled a pink stocking, pointed her toes, and starting at the ankles slowly rolled the hose onto her foot. She blew Kate a kiss. "I contacted the Chamber of Commerce. There are several community groups and sororities in the area. According to the bureau, they are always looking for someone to come and speak. And, there is a writer's group in the area and a coffee/book store."

Kate jumped up from her chair. "Okay, let's start with the coffee shop/book stores and the sororities. Forget the writers' group. Maybe I'll run into some old classmates who will tell me what in the hell is going on around here. But, schedule some time in between. We need to visit your apartment in Tampa. Now that Pops is settled in his apartment, we should be able to come and go a little more."

"You just don't want to lose track of Will, your flight attendant."

"He may be a big asset, Susie. He's very smart, he meets plane loads of people, and he's very cute. Why wouldn't I stay in touch?"

"You're preaching to the choir, sweetie. I've been nagging you for months to get back into the dating game, Kate. Back to the newspaper article, what are you going to do?"

"I'm going to play along like I never saw this article. Let's see what kind of deal I can make with the firm who wins awards for acquiring elderly people's estates."

"I just don't understand why you would lease the property you will someday inherit."

Kate jumped at Susie, her hands pretending to strangle her. "Because, I'm the Trustee, that's why!"

Susie jumped and laughed. "You scared me! You might have a career in acting yet. Of course, you don't have the dragon breath either."

"Seriously, Susie, if it takes the strain off Pop's account and gets Grandma Helen's affairs settled, I will play their game for now. Pops is so stressed, he can't think of anything else except the fishing cabin. He wants to go fishing before winter. With Grandma being sick for the previous five years, he's had no time."

"But wouldn't an attorney pursuing someone's trust be a breach of ethics?" Susie clipped her stockings into the lacy garter belt.

"This entire town is in their own little rat race. I think most of them are clueless. As long as the town benefits, why should anyone be concerned?" Kate grinned and picked up her computer case. "I might call Reese and have him run it by his judge."

"You enjoy torturing that poor bastard."

"No, I don't Susie. I like his friendship. I hope I'm not torturing him."

The doorbell rang, and Kate opened the door to two girls dressed as nurses from the 1920's, gorgeous blondes with perfect ringlets of bouncy hair and giggles to match.

"Hi, I'm Kate, and on my way out, but you ladies have fun."

Kate waved the nurses in and then waved at Susie. "They look authentic to me, Susie, but you might want to add a little color to the picture. Blondes have more fun, but we don't want to look like we're from L.A. Maybe the ladies know someone—not blonde, beautiful and a cookie cutter of you."

"You're right, Kate, we are obnoxiously white."

"Hey Susie, how about a party? You said you found my old yearbooks in the storage facility, how bout we invite the girls from my class? If I make a list, can you track down the ones who are local?"

"Why just women?" Susie pouted her pink lips.

"We need information—not boyfriends. I bet these new nurses will help."

"Sure, why not, isn't it in our job description?" The shorter of the two new recruits replied.

"Okay, I'm off to write my next best-selling novel. You ladies have fun. Susie, don't tell everything you know."

CHAPTER THIRTEEN

THE PLAN

K ate pulled into the parking lot of the cafe to grab dinner. Born and raised in the Midwest, she loved familiar places. The small diner located east of town was her new secret, writing hideout. She saw patrons in the yellow glow of the restaurant and the waitress clearing tables. It reminded her of the place in Georgia where she worked and hid when she was on the run for the murder charge.

Kate's phone rang, and she answered immediately. "Hi Pops."

"Katrina, this is your grandfather, I'm moving back to the nursing home. I'm sorry I troubled you to get me this apartment, but I don't like it here. I'm lonely, I miss my friends."

"Pops, listen, I was just going to grab a salad, can I bring you a cheeseburger?" *What's gotten into him now? That sounded like a script.*

"No, I've eaten, I'm tired, and I just want to go to bed. Your friend Harriett at the nursing home got me approved for Medicaid. They'll take my social security benefits for the rent. I'll receive food and board and an allowance of $25 per month. That's all I need."

"Medicaid—Pops, does that mean you don't have any money?" Kate flushed with anger, but tried to keep her tone calm. "Pops, we're a team now. You'll get some money from probate. There were assets not in the trust. Let's talk about this, I'll run over."

"I've made up my mind, Katrina. I've never really lived alone. I'm too old. The nursing home has activities, bingo, exercises. I've been a selfish old fool to bring you back here."

"Pops, my life's here now, you're not getting rid of me. I'm planning renovations for the cabin. Who have you been talking to?"

"Katrina, I'm tired, I'm going to bed now. Good night."

Kate heard the click of the phone, sat in the car for a moment and stared at the restaurant. *What the bloody hell am I going to do now?*

She jumped when she heard pecking on the window of the vintage Dodge Charger. She locked the door and grabbed her flashlight to defend herself. When she looked up, she found Reese Matthews grinning at her.

Kate opened the car door, pushing the big man out of her way. "You scared the hell out of me, whatta you doin' here?" She grabbed her purse and computer.

"Changed vehicles again, huh? I just finished a bite to eat."

"Are you following me, Reese?"

"Well, yes and no."

"Damn it, Reese, what gives you the right?" Kate stepped up onto the curb, hoping to be more face to face with the Chief for the confrontation. It didn't help. "I've got enough problems without you stalking me!"

"I'm not stalking you. I can explain, but you should calm down."

"Calm down! That's the last thing a man should ever say to a woman—ever."

"Okay, let's start over, can I buy you a cup of coffee or dinner?"

"No, you can't buy me anything, leave me alone."

Reese turned toward his truck as Kate changed her mind. "But, I could use some company." She walked over to the door of the cafe, opened it and motioned for the big man to go through.

"Thank you, Kate."

Once inside, she pointed to the corner of the restaurant. A small sign on a table in the corner read, "Reserved for Kate." As they passed the cash register, Kate recognized someone. "Don Armstrong, long time no see." She grinned and patted the man on his back.

"I can't talk to you," Don said.

"How's your nose?"

The attorney reached up and touched his nose. Kate laughed. "I'm not gonna punch you again." Kate passed by the attorney and joined Matthews at her reserved table. She looked up and saw the attorney gawking at them.

"Yes, Don, I'm meeting the Chief of Police for dinner," Kate shouted across the diner. The attorney left the restaurant without taking his change. The waitress threw the extra bills into the tip jar and signaled a "thumbs up" to Kate.

Matthews stood waiting for Kate to sit down. She swung her computer into the booth before he joined her. "You're pretty feisty tonight." He grinned at the young woman across from him.

Kate wore a blue shirt dress which accented her brown eyes, tennis shoes without socks, and she moved like a teenager.

"Are you working on a new novel?"

"Yes, Reese, and you're depicted as the villain again. Why are you following me?"

"I grabbed dinner and saw the sign, "Reserved for Kate." I thought it might be you, so I waited a few extra minutes, not stalking, just hopin' to run into you."

Kate rolled her eyes. "Okay, but, I'm in a bad mood, so if I seem snarky, it's because I am."

"Well, in that case, this can wait until another time." Reese started to scooch out of the booth.

"Scared of a girl, Chief?"

The waitress came with Kate's tea, "This is all I want for right now, Nellie, I can't eat, I feel a little sick."

Reese studied Kate, "What's wrong, you always eat. Has something happened?" The tactical cop would not speak again until she answered.

"Pops called tonight and said he wanted to leave his nice apartment and go back to the nursing home. He said he talked to the director, and they can get him a bed on Medicaid. Reese, that means he doesn't have any money. I'm just sick about it."

"Is that what you're so worried about—you think your grandfather's broke?" Reese laughed, his shoulders shook, and he shook his head. "He's playing you, Kate, he likes the attention and the sympathy. He's got you right where he wants you. He has money. Think about it."

Kate's icy glare melted into big tears. "Don't make fun of me. You didn't see them, Reese. The attorney and the accountant—they're like sharks. I'm not sure they couldn't con me out of my money. I think he's old. He wanted to be part of the boy's club. Everybody likes belonging to something. It's basic human law. It looks like Grandma gave away most of their money to some ungrateful, damn charities.

"I doubt it. I've known your grandfather—what, seven years? He's sharp. If I were you, I would check his hidey hole—perhaps a bank box. It's there somewhere. Look for cash, old coins and gold. He's got money. Your grandfather's a sly old fox. Don't worry about his money."

She sat for a moment staring out the window. Tear drops fell onto the table as she remembered how she had found Pops in the nursing home. "He doesn't even have a credit card. He used his card at the gas station and the accounting firm had cancelled it. Never mind, you're right, of course, you're right." She wiped away tears with the back of her hand. "I have been so worried. He's so frail. Pops did the best he could for me. Now it's my turn, but he doesn't make it easy."

"Why should he? It's called pay back."

She laughed. "I guess you're right, what goes around comes around."

The waitress came over, filled her tea, and poured him coffee.

"Nellie, how about pie? Do you want a piece of pie, Reese?" She did not wait for him to answer. "Two pieces of cherry pie, one with ice cream, please, Nellie."

"I guess that's settled." Reese grinned.

"I bet he put it in my trust fund."

"A trust fund brat? I'm surprised. How did my investigators not find your money?" Reese's brow furrowed as he stared at Kate.

"Missed something, eh?" Kate laughed. "Oh easy, my name on my birth certificate is Mary Kathleen Anderson. Pops called me Katrina Anne, and that's how he enrolled me in school. The trust is in her name— my name. I've never touched it, Pops always transferred the money into his account and then into mine. It does blur the cop trace, doesn't it?"

"Go on, there's more," Reese sipped his coffee.

"Susie found the statements in the storage facility. She can't understand this small-town stuff—bizarre, but true. My parents named me, Pops decided to call me something different. I didn't even know until I attended college. Isn't it odd? My grandfather changing my name after my parents' plane crashed? There was a hundred thousand dollars deposit from the plane's insurance company and another hundred thousand in life insurance. But, the bulk of the trust fund was sent to the bank in untraceable currency…"

"Just some quick addition, you're worth over a million bucks?"

"Without the new farm. Like I said, Pops manages it. I guess I should learn how to do that. Maybe that plot line will be my next book!"

Nellie gave Reese the stink eye. When he looked up, she smiled and said, "Here's your pie, sweetie, who gets the ice cream?"

"He does. Thanks, Nellie, this looks wonderful." Kate stared at her pie.

Reese dug in, but before taking a bite, he said, "Did Susie ask for a raise when she saw the bank statement?"

"She did. It was hysterical, you should have been there. She's so dramatic, she threw a real hissy fit. I told her I was saving the money for law school." Kate laughed a big, shaking belly laugh. "She'll get over it."

The diner was empty except for a cook and Nellie who was counting money at the register. The lights in the other corner had been turned down low. Reese took his last bite of pie-à la mode, sipped his coffee and said, "I have the murder weapon."

"What? You have my gun? The Sheriff's Department wouldn't release it to me. I guess the investigation is not closed, it's not open—it's pending. What the hell does that mean, Chief? How did you get the gun?"

"It means, they can't find the gun. And, I obtained the weapon like all people who have things that don't belong to them."

"Ooooh…you stole it? Did you leave a trail?"

He gave her the look. "No, and you don't want to know how I commandeered it."

"Are you going to give it to me?"

Reese put his fork on his plate and pushed them aside. "What are you going to do with it?"

"I'm gonna plant it. Maybe create a domino effect—let's test the theory about what goes around comes around.

CHAPTER FOURTEEN

AMBULANCE RIDE

The ambulance pulled in front of Harlow's restaurant, lights and sirens blaring. The red and blue strobes and siren came to a sudden halt. Two paramedics dressed in green scrubs unloaded the stretcher and hurried into the restaurant. The converted nightclub had most of the original decorations. Inside, the business appeared dark for 9:00 a.m., the only light coming from a stain glass window on the wall near the entrance. A hostess, with perfectly coifed beehive hair and manicured nails, pointed over to the middle of the room.

"That old man was walking…and…and he just collapsed into the chair. He's a regular every Thursday morning."

"You're not okay, Ted, we've called an ambulance." The paramedic heard a woman addressing the man. He stopped to let his eyes adjust to the dark setting.

"Don't call Kate," the old man whispered to the woman.

The paramedic rushed to the patient and said, "Hi, my name is Derik, can you give me your name?"

"Theodore Anderson." The old man gasped. "I'm fine, I just got a little dizzy, I want to go home."

"How old are you, Theodore?"

"Ninety-two."

"Theodore, here's what we're going to do. We're going to load you into the ambulance, check all your vital signs, get some information from you, and notify your doctor. If you check out, we will let your friend take you home, but you can't drive. Does that sound like a good plan to you? You need a little oxygen."

"Yes." The old man attempted a smile. As they were loading the ambulance, a vintage, blue Dodge Charger roared up next to the ambulance. A good-looking young woman jumped out, leaving her door ajar, and ran to the back of the ambulance.

"Pops, are you okay? Is he okay?" She searched the paramedic's face.

"We need to check him out. He's responding and we're getting his vitals, if you can give us a minute. My name is Derik. We're going to close the door for a minute, but unless there is an emergency we'll get right back to you."

Kate stepped back and allowed the paramedic to close the door. She ran over to her car, grabbed her purse, and shut the door. She paced back and forth behind the ambulance.

Within minutes a group came out of the restaurant. Kate recognized the woman as Diana Birdsell. "What happened? You were with Pops, right?"

"We were eating breakfast and your grandfather and Bob started bantering insults like always, but then—your grandfather got up and said he didn't feel well. I followed him because he never just gets up and leaves. I'm glad I did, because he collapsed, and I was able to catch him."

"Thank you, Diana. Pops and Bob still eat breakfast together?"

"Well, yes, every Thursday. Is there a reason we shouldn't?"

"I'm shocked. Did you know they are embroiled in lawsuits regarding Grandma Helen's estate?"

"We had no idea."

"Neither of them talks about it?"

The restaurant door opened again. Bob, Kate's step-uncle, lumbered out. Dressed in bib overalls and a long-sleeved checkered shirt, his attire had not changed in the last six years. Kate noticed he was a good fifty pounds lighter. At seventy, he looked almost her grandfather's age.

"I hope the old fucker dies." Bob glared at Kate.

Kate realized Bob, once a powerful brute and bully, must be ill. The disease that ravaged his kidneys was taking a huge toll on the rest of his body.

The ambulance door swung open. Kate ignored Uncle Bob and jumped in.

"You can't come in here."

"Too late, Derik."

Pops pointed at Kate and said, "That's my…"

"Pops, how are you?" An oxygen mask hid most of his face. Kate studied his eyes. Although he was pale, he didn't seem in distress. He blinked twice at her, like he knew a secret code, so she blinked back at him. She tried to hold his hand, but Pops struggled to get something out of his pocket, IV attached.

"Pops, what do you need?"

"My billfold." He took a deep breath. "I owe Bob five dollars. I can't die owing that son of a bitch money."

Kate laughed, "I think you had a dizzy spell. Don't worry, I'll pay him."

"Today," Pops said.

Derik interrupted, "Kate, we're taking him to the hospital. He might have fainted, but at his age, he should be checked out. We talked him into taking a ride with us. It was a hard sell, but we got the job done. He says he's never had an ambulance ride."

"Don't let him fool you, he received one of the first quadruple bypasses in St. Luke's in 1989. He's been in ambulances and a helicopter. He's been under a great deal of stress the last six months."

Pops lifted his finger in the air, "I don't remember any of that, I didn't lie."

"Of course, you didn't." Kate said with a grin. "Pops, you're going to be okay, I'll follow you to the hospital— enjoy your ride." She jumped out of the vehicle.

"Wait, just a minute, Kate, does he have a DNR?"

"DNR? Do not resuscitate? No, I don't think so. No, I'm sure of it."

"Check in at admitting, they'll need information from you."

Kate turned and looked at the breakfast club, minus her Uncle Bob. She scanned the area and saw Bob and his wife, Billie, backing their new Cadillac out of a handicap parking space. Kate reached in her bag and grabbed a five-dollar bill. She jogged over to the car and smashed the note onto the windshield and yelled, "Pops says he owes you this."

Bob punched the brake. He rolled down the window, and Kate flicked the bill into his lap.

"You, you nosy little bitch, you'll never live at that cabin." He backed out of the parking space.

Kate turned her back on her step uncle. *We'll see about that.* She hopped back into her car and called Susie, relating what happened to Pops.

"Is he okay?"

"I think so, they are taking him to the hospital. He was cussing. I doubt he'd be cussing if he were dying. Scared the hell out of me. I'm on the way to the hospital."

"Those police scanner things really come in handy, don't they? I can't believe you could recognize what was going on from the chatter I heard in the background."

"Years of practice."

"I'm coming to the hospital."

"You better check your schedule, busy girl. Don't you have our party to plan? The hospital will be all red tape and lots of medical questions."

"You still want me to plan the party?"

"Sure, I think he's fine, and as I said before, people talk at parties. Maybe we can pry some mouths open with booze. Plus, Pops loves a good party. It will be a good diversion for him."

"You're taking this lightly, Kate. He's ninety-two and has been under a great deal of stress. He's lost his wife, his home."

"I really think he's just dehydrated. We can always cancel."

"Okay, I'll bring the invitations and you can help me address them."

"You're kidding, right, Miss Techie? We're not sending out invitations, we'll send an Evite."

"Oh crap. Sometimes, I really understand all the blonde jokes. I'll bring the computer and your yearbook, we can stalk some people on Facebook, and send out an Evite for the best party this town has seen in a long while."

"Susie, before you come, would you search Pop's trust documents and see if you find instructions? You know, in the event he cannot decide things for himself? Power of Attorney, Medical Power of Attorney, that kind of thing."

"Of course. I was organizing them just yesterday."

"I also need some clothes, I ran out in my yoga gear and feel quite conspicuous."

"A little naked, are you?" Susie teased.

"One more thing. Email our computer geek. Ask him to check Yelp and all the other business sites. I need the name of the meanest, bitchiest, most outrageous female attorney money can buy."

CHAPTER FIFTEEN

THE ENEMY OF MY ENEMY

J ennifer Doyle glared at the envelope, sat down and emptied her arms, spewing file folders, envelopes and an adding machine across the desk. They tumbled into the penholder and it fell to the floor. She snatched up the envelope and tore it open. A check fell out, fluttering to the desk, then the floor. Jennifer bent over and picked it up, examining the check. Her large eyes bulged as she glowered at it.

In perfect black penmanship, Kate Anderson had written a check to the trust for two thousand dollars— a year's rent, for the taxes and insurance on her two-hundred-acre property. One day she would inherit it, but for now H.O.G.G. had all the power.

Jennifer Doyle hated Kate Anderson. She hated everything about her, especially how men stopped talking when Kate entered the room. No one stopped talking when Jennifer walked into a room. Jennifer and Kate, high school classmates, reunited when Kate brought her grandfather into the accountant's office to learn about her grandmother's trust. The accounting firm and the attorney believed Kate was safely out of the way, that the old man had no one—except his chronically ill wife. Taking the money in the form of a trust document would be easy. Theodore Anderson was a nice man, eager to please the smooth-talking accountant. He wanted to make his wife happy. She decided to leave certain assets to the community: thirty thousand dollars to three charities and the same amount to each of three stepchildren from her previous marriage.

I wonder if the old lady is rolling over in her grave. Most of her money has been given away to charity. Jennifer's thoughts were interrupted by the boss's demand.

"Come in here."

She jumped when she heard the accountant bark into the intercom. *What in the hell does he want?*

Jennifer looked like a large praying mantis—her small face ended in a heart-shape, her large eyes magnified with thick round glasses. Somehow, she was camouflaged by her own skin. Her wardrobe consisted of tan pants, tan blouses and tan or green jackets. She often wondered if she were invisible. Tall and thin, she moved in slow motion. When she spoke, she often cleared her throat, and cleared it again, hoping someone would notice her.

She grabbed her steno book and left the mess on her desk and floor. With her feet stuffed into expensive sandals a size too small, she clopped down the hall and into her boss' office.

The accountant sat at his desk wearing a pink golf shirt and tan pants. *Golf day, thank God*. She cleared her throat. He ignored her.

He finally asked, "Was that a check from Kate Anderson in the mail?" The accountant looked up and eyed Jennifer with a shark-like stare. "Did the attorney settle with her to allow her to rent that cabin?"

"How would I know?" Shocked at her own rudeness, she took a step back, distancing herself from the accountant, then added more softly, clearing her throat, "Yes, there was a check."

The accountant glared at Jennifer. "How much was it?"

"Two thousand dollars. Noted for rent and taxes."

The accountant settled back in his chair and studied her. "I'm sorry, Jennifer, of course, it's not your fault. I'm yelling at you instead of the attorney."

Jennifer did not answer and waited to be dismissed.

"How is your grandmother?"

"My grandmother? What do you mean my grandmother?"

Jennifer tried to study the accountant's face, but quickly looked away, in fear.

"Jennifer, please, I'm a little hard to work for, but we truly want to be a family here. Is there anything the firm can do for your grandmother?"

"No—my father takes care of all her business."

"What's your father's name again? Why don't you set an appointment for him to see me? We should make sure all of her affairs are in order."

Jennifer took a step over an invisible line in the doorway and yelled at the man. "Do you think I'm stupid? I'm not blind to what goes on around here. You believe you can soothe her into signing the last page of a document giving away her hard-earned money? You and that despicable lawyer—stay away from my grandmother."

The accountant stood up and pointed toward her office. "Go back to your office and get your work done. I will not tolerate your tone. Trust me when I say, I will fire you."

Jennifer turned and walked down the hall. She almost glided. *Yes, you heard me, asshole. It is different when it's my family.* She returned to her office and picked up the check with the return address of Florida. *The enemy of my enemy is my friend. Who knows where Kate Anderson is staying while she's in town?* She picked up the phone and called Harriett at the nursing home. *I should be ashamed of myself, watching this happen to other good families.*

"Harriett, this is Jennifer. Where is Kate Anderson staying?"

"Get right to the point, Jennifer—no 'hello, how are you?'"

"I'm sorry, Harriett, having a bad day here. The men haven't left for their golf game and the accountant is insufferable."

"C'mon Jennifer, I was teasing you. I visited your grandma this morning. She seems to be doing a bit better today. It's so weird you asked, Kate is throwing a party and we're invited."

"I'm also looking for a job."

"Really, it can't be that bad, your job pays well, especially for this town."

"It's better than being fired. What do you mean, we're invited?"

"Our high school class, but just the girls. She sent me a cute little Evite saying she would like for some of us girls to get together. It'll be so much fun."

"I've seen her, too, but she didn't recognize me—no surprise. I hate Kate Anderson, she thinks she's a celebrity in this town."

"She *is* a celebrity and her party will be the best. You must have some interest in her or you wouldn't have called me about her. Please come with me. She has rented that cute little place above the attorney's office on Main Street. We will get some good gossip. It's just girls, so Michael will have to find something else to do that night. I'll forward you the Evite. It says *Pass the Word,* so we can make it our own party."

"Okay, I'll go. Please tell grandma I will be out to see her today. Goodbye for now."

Jennifer straightened her desk, rolled over to her computer, and started typing.

"Anonymous source says…" she erased it and started again. She went back and forth…typing, deleting, typing again. She deleted every word, chose not to save the document, deleted her history and shut down her computer. *Who knows what the IT guys can find.*

Jennifer pulled a small greeting card from her collection and penned in blue scrolling ink:

The answer to your questions, I will give you a clue.
There is a group called The Founders -- despicable men.
They meet at 7:00 p.m. on Law Day in the old bank building.
And some of them play golf on Wednesday mornings at the Country Club.

She placed the clue in a little pink envelope, labeled it "Kate Anderson", and stuffed it in her purse.
I can leave this clue at the party. No one will know it is me.

CHAPTER SIXTEEN

REFLECTION

Kate paced outside her grandfather's hospital room in the modern building until she settled herself near a window and looked outside. She viewed the new soccer stadium blazing with purple and gold fields and bright bleachers which appeared to glow in the dark. A large eagle was stamped in the field. She could also see the newly constructed restaurant and bowling alley adjacent to the movie theater. Out of view were the golf course and the launch site for the new middle school. The hospital was breaking ground for a new prayer garden, a million-dollar park for prayer. The bulldozers and large equipment cast long shadows on the ground.

She felt his presence as he came up behind. She turned. "Hello, Reese—thanks for coming."

"How is he?" She stood in the hallway and the awkward dance of hug-no hug standoff began. Law enforcement shake hands and sometimes pat each other on the back—they don't hug.

"He's sleeping now. They're keeping him overnight to run a few tests. He might have been a little dehydrated from drinking with an old buddy yesterday. They started at the nursing home and ended up at the bar. His buddy has a golf cart and the assisted living center is a couple blocks from that new bar." Kate laughed and shook her head.

"I like your new look," Reese grinned.

Kate looked down at herself and blushed, realizing she was still in her yoga pants and skimpy Nike shirt. "Susie has me doing yoga. She says I'm way too uptight."

"Naw. Not you."

"Can you believe this town, Reese? When I fled from here six years ago, none of these buildings existed. Was it even planned? Cows grazed all around us. This little farming community in the middle of nowhere struggled. The farmers had money—the ones that survived the 80's, but they kept it in their own pockets."

"Maybe the old guard died off. Maybe this generation wants to build a place for their kids. The kids were all fleeing this place six years ago. Susie coming out?"

"Or, maybe, it's a criminal enterprise. Oh—let's not talk about it. Susie…uh, she's bringing me food and a pillow and probably packing me a week's worth of clothes. I'm staying tonight and will be here to speak to the doctor in the morning. She's also been given the assignment to interrogate Pops. It's gonna be interesting."

"And there she is, right on cue," Reese smiled.

Susie entered the waiting room, dressed like she were going out to a high-class restaurant in New York City, in a short red dress, her long blonde hair straightened. She strutted in four-inch heels. "Hi Sweetie, Momma's here."

"Perfect timing, we were just talking about you," Kate said.

"Of course you were, what else do you two have to talk about?" Susie eyed Reese.

"I was leaving, I thought I would check on Kate."

"Oh, don't leave on my account. I love your company."

"As I enjoy yours. Duty calls. I have a roster to make out for next week and a budget to complete."

Susie waved her hand in front of him, "Boring, boring, how can you make things sound so boring?"

Kate watched the verbal exchange between Reese and Susie. A smile played on her lips. *They would be perfect together.* "Thanks for coming, Reese. It meant a lot to me. I will tell Pops you stopped by."

"Tell him I want to go fishing."

"Okay, I will."

A nurse stepped through the doorway to Pop's room and Kate followed her in. She checked his machines and wrote in his chart.

"Can *you* tell me anything?"

"He's pretty tuckered, do you want to wake him for dinner?"

"Absolutely, he's recently lost about thirty pounds."

"All right." The woman gave a big sigh. "Choose from the menu over there. Use the telephone and call in your order. You can also order from the guest menu. If he wakes up, or if you wake him up—press the nurse's button. He's a fall risk and we should help him to the bathroom."

The nurse attempted to exit. Kate blocked the door and stopped her from leaving.

"Where do I get the form to have him sign a medical release authorizing me to see his records?"

"Go to the nurses' station."

"Can you tell me anything?"

"He's old, he's worn out, his diet is probably bad."

"Okay, so I will order him some food and hit the call button after I wake him up. You here all night?"

"Ending my shift at 6:00 p.m., then Nurse Cammie takes over."

"I'll wait until six then." Kate ignored the woman's glare. She looked at her grandfather who appeared to be sleeping peacefully. She heard laughter in the hallway, Susie exchanging jokes with Reese. Kate waited a minute until she could hear Reese's footsteps.

"Hey, girl, thanks for coming. Sorry for the quick exit, I thought I would get some info. She's a real piece of work, Nurse Ratchet, she is."

Susie shook her head. "What's the plan here? Other than you need to change your clothes." She wagged her finger at Kate.

"I know, what did you bring me?"

114

"Your usual, jeans and sweatshirt. Really, Kate, your wardrobe is down to bare bones. Why don't we do some online shopping tonight? You certainly don't look like a woman worth a million bucks."

"Oh stop, give it a rest. Enough with the teasing. What do you want me to do? Put an ad in the paper? Kate Anderson, the richest single woman in Kingseat, Missouri. I promise, shopping will come, and yes, you deserve a raise and a bonus, but give me some time to figure it out."

"All right, I'll stop. Besides, I should tell you—I asked Reese to come back. I need him as back up if Pops won't talk. I told him this was my first undercover job. That phrase always cracks me up. I need some training from our very special Chief of Police." She winked at Kate.

"Susie, you know it's all clear for you to make any play you want with Reese. You do know that? I swear, he's a friend—only a friend. We had our little cat fight about him, years ago, but you understand he's not right for me."

"Are you sure?"

"You two are gaggy cute together."

Susie made a face. "I know, Kate, we *are* cute together."

"What? That's your mock remorseful face." Kate laughed. "I get it now, boy, I'm slow. Well, I've told you both a million times. Oh, lots of things are making sense now. That's why he waited to talk to me at the diner. Enough of that—don't think you're getting out of

115

telling me everything, but right now we're on a time schedule. Pops will eat and then fall asleep. Here's the plan. I'll order him some dinner. While he's eating, just pretend you are on a date with a handsome movie star and grill him. Think of it as a game. He will."

"And, if that doesn't work I'm going to tell him Reese Matthews is coming in here and putting the thumb screws on him."

"Okay." Kate laughed. "What have you been binging on—Netflix, old time Mob movies? If that doesn't work, bribe him with the whiskey. Did you bring the flask?

"Of course."

"We can set up my phone to record it?"

"Yes, Kate."

"Here's the list of questions we need to ask him. Pretend you are on a Vlog and this is your script. You're a natural, Susie. You've got about twenty minutes to prepare, and bonus—Cammie's coming in at six. I'll try to get some information out of Pops' new nurse."

CHAPTER SEVENTEEN

THE ART OF THE DEAL

P ops sat up in the bed with his oversized hospital gown askew. His bare shoulder showed a once muscled man, now a skeleton with skin. A few freckles popped out, but he was as white as the sheet. Oxygen ran to his nose. His blue veined hands were opaque and freckled. An IV ran up his arm to a saline solution hanging in a bag above his head. In contrast, his brown eyes twinkled as he watched the pretty young woman set up his tray.

"It looks like we have soft food for you, Theodore. It's chicken noodle soup, cherry Jell-O and pudding. Kate ordered every flavor of pudding. She's changing her clothes, then she'll be in. She was embarrassed in her yoga gear," Susie said.

"Wow, you're a real-looker, you know."

"Oh, you are a sweet talker, Theodore Anderson." Susie spoke in her best British accent.

"Best looking nurse I've ever seen."

"You do know it's me—Susie?"

"Kate got you doing her dirty work for her?" The sly old man's eyes slanted as he studied the attractive woman.

"Not dirty work, Theodore. You know I enjoy your company and care about you. But, yes, she thought you would talk to me. We're still confused how this trust turned out the way it did." Susie took the lid off the chicken soup. "Yum—smells exactly like hospital food."

Theodore picked up his spoon and tapped the top of the banana pudding cup. She opened it and gave it to him. He took a bite, smiled, and then tapped the chocolate pudding with his spoon. She opened it for him.

"Fun little game we're playing. You still don't have a poker face, Susie."

"Poker is it? You want to play cards? I have them in my purse. I win, you talk to me. You win, well Theodore, I go home—but what would *you* win?"

He took another bite of his pudding, set it down, and started talking.

"I know you've been going through our files and you know about all the trips to the attorney's office. Helen liked Howard, and it was something we did after we paid our taxes. Our financial guy advised us to review our wills once a year as we got older. I thought of the attorney as a friend. When Helen broke her hip, and she came home, I thought it was nice having the attorney come to the house. His wife made the best peach pie,

Helen's favorite. He brought me expensive booze. I don't like expensive booze but figured someone would drink it."

Susie shrugged her shoulders and then nodded in agreement. Theodore went on. "Well, then she broke her back and something else, uh, her pelvis. Before long, she broke her back again. It was awful. She hit her head and blood went everywhere." Theodore shook his head and took another bite of pudding.

"Our friends stopped coming to see us. Some moved away, closer to their kids. Some got sick themselves. The attorney started talking about how nice it would be for Helen to leave some money to the city. Howard said, 'Just let me draw up an outline, and I'll come back, and we can review it—you can make any changes you want.' Helen never liked any of it. It was me—all me." He took his spoon and tapped his heart with it. Tears filled his eyes. "Now your turn, tell me about Katrina."

Susie moved over closer to the old man. "She's published her first book, working on her second. I'm her publicist. I do all the hard work, don't you know?" Susie shot Pops a smile and patted his hand. "I get a nice cut of the profits, and the book is doing great, especially here in Missouri. It needs more marketing, but we've been busy. You've kept us pretty busy."

"Is she seeing anyone? Is she seeing that cop?"

"No, she doesn't like him. He's much too old for Kate. And he's been married and has a son. She has no intention of ever being a stepmother. Besides, I think that 'ship has sailed,' as they say. She does like somebody else, but you talk now."

Susie opened the butterscotch pudding. The old man began talking as if remembering was physically painful. "Howard, the attorney, drew up the paperwork for what they called a foundation in her honor. It was laying on the table one day, when my old friend, Warren came over to visit. He's five years older than me. He told us that Howard was just out to get our money. He said he knew several people who gave away their fortunes. He didn't want it to happen to us. He reminded me I had a granddaughter to inherit the money. Truthfully, I was so wrapped up in getting Helen taken care of, the bills paid and taking her to the hairdresser and the nail salon, I hadn't thought about Kate or her inheritance. That sounds wrong—I thought about her and prayed for her every day, but I didn't think about her inheritance or our legacy to her." Theodore paused and caught his breath.

"That night after Warren left, Helen said she wanted to leave everything to me. She wanted Bob to be able to farm the land until he died. I went to the attorney the next morning. They drew up papers, Howard came out to the house, and she signed them. I thought she left me everything. That was August 15th. She died a couple weeks later."

Susie saw the old man's face darken, so she cut in. "Kate's seeing a guy named Will Johnson. He's very handsome, more her age, and has a great job with an airline. They both love to travel. He's very smart, an engineer. I've got a picture for you to see." Susie picked up her phone and showed Theodore a picture of Will and Kate standing inside the airport in Kansas City.

"Thank you, she looks happy. That's all I ever wanted was for her to be happy."

"Did you know Jean and I—my first wife—didn't know where Kate was when her parents' plane went down. Jean was frantic to find her. I buried my feelings with my son. I figured my son and his wife were good parents, they must've left Kate with someone safe. When we found Kate, she was such a busy, unhappy little thing. Never smiled, never really cried, just asked for her momma and daddy and puppy. Then, Jean died right before Thanksgiving. I think she died of a broken heart."

He looked down, shook his head, and then as if catching himself from falling into a deep black hole, he looked up and changed the subject. "I'm surprised she's interested in him considering he's a pilot and what happened to her parents."

"He's not a pilot, but he works for the airline. I don't think she meant to get involved with him. It started out as just a friendship, and I think it has rapidly evolved into a romance."

"How did they meet?"

"They met on the plane to come home here. She's gone down to meet him in Kansas City a few times. She doesn't tell much, as you well know." Susie crossed her eyes, attempting a funny face.

121

"Sounds like a Hallmark movie--maybe a Christmas movie." His eyes lit up again.

"Pops, you're a romantic—you like Hallmark movies? I think Kate's life is more like a Lifetime Women's Series movie—those are good, too. Please don't tell Kate I said that. She hates those movies. So, you married Helen shortly after your wife died."

"What choice did I have? I couldn't let Katrina go live with some stranger. I couldn't take care of her. My job was to make her tough, you understand that don't you?"

"You certainly did that, Pops—she's tough. With my screwed-up family, you two look like a Hallmark movie to me. But, tell me one more thing, how'd you wind up in the nursing home?"

"Well, let me think." He picked up the milk and took a swallow, dabbed his mouth with his napkin.

"The house went up for auction. Helen died before the closing. Like I said, I thought she left me everything. I got through the funeral fine, but after Kate left, I started drinking. I was supposed to be able to live in the house for life. I don't understand how I got so mixed up." Theodore threw up his hands. "I don't know, I was living in a nearly empty house. One day, the accountant banged on the door and told me I had to get out. He moved my things and arranged for me to go to the nursing home." Theodore shook his head. "So, you found my money?"

"Five hundred-seventy-five thousand dollars? Yes, we found it."

"I don't want to touch it. That's my legacy to Kate."

"Reese Matthews thinks you've got money hidden somewhere else."

The old man's eyes squinted and he studied her. "Matthews is a smart man. He came to see me a few times when Kate was on the run. I always thought he would come back and threaten me in an attempt to tell him where she was hiding, but he never did. I like him. I told him he would never find her." The old man pointed his spoon at Susie, "Aww, that's it, Susie, you like our Chief of Police, isn't that something?"

Susie laughed her musical laugh. "You are a sly one, aren't you, Theodore. Yes, it's true. I told Kate earlier."

Kate stuck her head in the door. "What have you two been up to?"

Pops pointed at Kate and scowled. "Katrina, get the nurse," he ordered. "I have to use the toilet. And turn on that TV, I think football's on."

CHAPTER EIGHTEEN

THE WITCH

Maureen Thompson, the attorney, left the courthouse wearing a black London Fog raincoat, a size too large for her ample frame. She drew the hood around her greying red hair and marched on, briefcase in hand. Following Kate's directions, she searched for the Dog Groomer's Shop and the door to Kate's apartment.

"Come in, get out of that wind. Thanks for walking over. We live upstairs." Kate ran up a flight of stairs and looked down at the woman who trudged up. When the woman reached the top of the stairs, Kate opened the door to her apartment.

"Welcome, let me take your coat. Can I get you something to drink?"

"Whatcha got? I'm Maureen Thompson by the way. Kate Anderson, I presume? If my client drinks, I drink. I must look a fright, I doubt you care." She attempted to pat and also fluff her unruly hair.

"Let's drink," Kate said, as she took the woman's coat and hung it on the hallway hook. "I can make a Martini, a Margarita, I have a nice red wine or — whiskey?"

"Straight up, Crown if you've got it." The woman made herself at home on a bar stool at the island in the kitchen.

"My kind of woman." Kate poured two fingers of warm liquid into a crystal whiskey glass and handed it to Ms. Thompson. "You come highly recommended by your clients—and not so recommended by ex-husband's. I like it." Kate joined the attorney at the island, they clinked their glasses together, and both took sips of the warm liquid.

"And, your reputation proceeds you: fleeing from a murder charge, writing several good journalism articles and a novel. I'm just gonna be straight with you, Revocable trusts, hate them. They should be against the law. It's a great way for elderly people to get fleeced. If it wasn't for the mess of our probate system, no one would use them. I would write a bill for our state senator, but it's not really my job. They cause nasty messes."

"I didn't know anything about them—but I'm in a nasty mess now."

"Every damn attorney in this town is a dick. You've found that out, I expect."

Kate laughed, "I already knew it, but I feel a whole new pain."

"Why do you want to sue? You don't need the money." The attorney looked around the room. "Nice, modest apartment, but I suspect this is temporary and you are quite self-sufficient."

"It doesn't mean I want the attorneys to jingle their pockets with my grandmother's money. Or, for the damn ungrateful charities to have any of it. Besides, they robbed my grandfather of his love story. He's a romantic. Tough as nails, lived through the depression, wars. He lost his only son and his daughter-in-law—they were my parents—then his first wife, my grandmother. And, eight weeks ago, his second wife, my Grandma Helen, passed away. They had a different kind of love, a friendship of sticking it out and through thick and thin. His drinking, her illnesses. No one should be robbed of their love story—especially at the age of ninety-two. His memories are all he has."

"He has you." The attorney smiled and seemed to soften into a warm motherly type. A woman who rarely showed herself with her clients.

"My grandfather and I are strangers. I'm not sure he recognizes me or knows my name half the time. 'There you are!' That's what he says—to me and everyone else who enters his room. We're generations apart. We never had much in common except blood, duty, and memories of my parents. He believed his job was to make me tough. I just wanted to sit on his lap. Don't get me wrong, I left any anger and resentment on the road in Georgia, where some extremely nice people babied me, and counseled me."

"You want to sue because he was robbed of his love story. I'll be damned," she slapped the bar. "You're a romantic, too, Kate Anderson."

"'Evil exists if good men stand by and do nothing,' might be a more truthful answer," Kate said.

"Edmund Burke, 'evil exists if good WOMEN stand by and do nothing.' A lawsuit could take years and lots of hassle. Like I said, I hate revocable trusts."

"You've already decided to take the case, or you wouldn't be here. You employ a sharp paralegal. She can do most of the work. It will be just another lawsuit. Besides, I'm one of the best documenters in the State of Missouri. I have the attorney and the accountant on tape and I have Pops on video. Want another drink?"

"We can't use the tape in court."

"I know, but it will sound great in a deposition."

"You're willing to go through depositions?"

"Of course! I love court. I'm an excellent witness. I've rented my apartment in Tampa, so I'm here. I attended all the court hearings from Pop's case. No representative from H.O.G.G. ever bothered to come to court." Kate said the word "hog" like she had a bad taste in her mouth. "Their office is literally right across the street from the courthouse. The judge didn't even require an appearance. I suspect my attorney will keep me out of court until I testify." She sipped her drink and studied the attorney.

"You understand, your grandfather does not have a good case. I'm sorry, but it's true. He's just too frail and old to make it through a trial. But, you probably do."

"I'll make myself available. You want another drink?"

"Naw, I'm going to grab a bite to eat. You wanna come?" The attorney pulled out her lipstick and mirror and started redrawing her red lips.

"The point of us meeting in my apartment was to not be seen in public. Small town, people talk, more of a surprise attack. Let me order some food from the diner."

"You're not suing for revenge? Not that I really care, but it helps me know how I can best please the client. " Maureen studied the younger woman.

Kate's voice lowered as she leaned in across the table. "You ever been invited to a revenge party?" Kate looked the attorney straight in the eye. "I didn't think so, you don't make the cut. Revenge is something best done alone."

The attorney laughed, "Don't call me if you get arrested. I'm not a defense attorney. Your stare makes me think you shot that man."

"I won't." Kate finished her drink and poured another round.

"I think you have three viable cases. But, let's talk about one. There's a property—it has the nice red barn. Until recently it was all one farm attached to yours. The trustee has surveyed it and it has been appraised. It's worth about three hundred thousand dollars. What's the status on your cabin and your farm?"

"So, you did your homework. I rented the cabin and ten acres from the trustee, best deal I could make. I signed my rights away to sue for the damages to the cabin. I don't care. We're going out there in a few days. It'll be a friggin' mess. It's been vacant for ten months. Mold and mice will take over a place in Missouri in a heartbeat. It made me sick to negotiate with the snakes, but Pops wants to go fishing and he needs to know I have possession of it."

"I usually like to start at the beginning, but it's not a problem. You understand I'll have to file suit against your grandmother's trust and the attorney."

"The trustee refused to use my grandmother's married name, so it makes no difference to me if we sue her trust. Regarding the rental agreement, I stumbled through it—I can also testify I tried to work it out with them. It's part of the plan."

"You're pretty smart, Kate." The attorney straightened her silk blouse and pushed the glass over to Kate.

"Why don't I order us some food? What would you like? The diner will deliver here in a jiff. I need to eat something and sober up. Pops gave me a big scare, I thought I lost him. He's in the hospital. He's busy this afternoon with therapy, but I'll have to go out there tonight."

"If you're ordering from the diner, I'll take a cheeseburger."

Kate ordered burgers and salads. "I would like to stagger the lawsuits. Punch them once, punch them twice, punch them again."

The attorney pointed at Kate, "I like you. I don't normally drink at lunch, but my husband asked me for a divorce this morning. Maybe these lawsuits are just what I need. Staggering the lawsuits may get sticky with the judge. He won't like it, but I do."

"And I like you—but I like your reputation more. Can you file something in court asking for a general accounting, so we can give them a little Christmas present? We should get Uncle Bob's deposition before, well—let's just say, while he's still really pissed and before he's dead. I hate to be crude, but he must be very ill. I've been drinking, that's my excuse for my rudeness."

"They've not given your grandfather an accounting?"

"Nope, and I want it public."

"Have you ever thought of going to law school?"

Kate laughed, "It's my grandfather's dream for me. I think there are more than three lawsuits."

The attorney whistled. "Okay then—we need to set up a time for you to come over to my office. I'll draw up paperwork for our agreement. No drinking." She pointed at Kate.

"Think about a percentage—since you're getting a divorce, maybe you want to keep your account balance low. A percentage gives you an incentive to rake in more money, it delays your pay-out and should make you more money," Kate grinned.

Susie opened the door with sacks of food. "I found your delivery man." She looked over at the middle-aged woman half-sitting, half-standing and leaning over the kitchen bar and at Kate leaning across the sink. "What's going on here? It's not even three in the afternoon and you both look sauced."

Kate held the nearly empty bottle of Crown, and they both answered, "too much whiskey."

"You've gotten so you'll drink with anybody, Kate."

"Hey, hey, I'm not just anybody," the attorney slurred, "I'm your friend's really bitchy soon-to-be divorced attorney." She pulled her hair straight up, and it stuck. "Maybe I'm the wicked witch! It is Halloween!"

CHAPTER NINETEEN

DNR

K ate tried to settle in the recliner in Pop's hospital room, but he snored, and she could not sleep. She paced the hallway of the new hospital. Her cowboy boots made a click-clack which echoed down the walls. At two in the morning Kate found the chapel. She opened the door, saw two small padded pews facing an altar. A massive cross hung on the wall and the fake stained-glass windows were filled with light. Blues, golds and reds outlined a picture of Christ in the garden. She made the sign of the cross, sat down in a pew, slid off her cowboy boots, and pulled her knees to her chest. A prayer-like state swept over her and she rested.

At 6:00 a.m. she startled awake, stretched, and pulled on her cowboy boots. She peeked in on Pops and walked down to the cafeteria. She grabbed a bowl of oatmeal, a cup of coffee, and dodged nurses in multi-colored scrubs as the hospital prepared for the shift change and the dawn of a new day.

❧ ❧ ❧

Kate opened the door to Pop's room. "Pops, what are you doing out of bed? They didn't want you to get up." She pointed at the sign which read "Fall Risk."

"I'm going home. I've been here two days and they're killing me."

"It may seem like a long time—but Pops, you've only been here overnight. What did you do, remove your IV?"

Kate recognized the look. His jaw was set like concrete—there was no use arguing with him. "Of course, you did. Let me see." She lifted his hand. A fragment of Kleenex stuck where his hand had bled.

"I've been gone a bit to get a bite to eat—how did you get dressed so fast? You'll have to sign papers. We can't just leave."

"Why not?"

"I'm not gonna argue with you. If they haven't found anything wrong with you, there's no reason for you not to go home."

Theodore struggled to get on his feet. He took a couple of steps and grabbed the bed.

"Pops, you need your cane and you need to eat breakfast. Let me order you something to eat and get you discharged properly. I'm sure Susie will bring your cane, but not quite this early."

Kate turned to look for the menu. Out of the corner of her eye she watched as he reached back, found the arm of the chair and sat down. She kept her back turned but read the menu: cold items, fruit, cereal, toast.

Pops interrupted. "Never mind that—order me two eggs, sunny side up, wheat toast, juice and coffee. Kate, what if this is my last day? I don't want to spend it here."

Kate repeated the breakfast order into the phone. She sat down on the other side of the room and looked out at the construction of the prayer garden. *How ironic. A one-million-dollar prayer garden and a closet for a chapel.* The two sat in silence and avoided looking at each other.

She heard the doctor in the hallway and stood. "Good morning, Mr. Anderson." He entered the room, stopped, searched for the patient, and then checked the chart. "What are you doing out of bed?"

Pops lit up like a Christmas tree. He sat straight and tall and smiled. "I'm perfect—and my granddaughter's driving me home."

"Mr. Anderson, we haven't finished your tests. Your heart stopped. We would like to consider you for a pacemaker and a defibrillator. To do that, we will have to run more tests."

"I just got dizzy. I want to go home."

"Mr. Anderson, we need to run more tests. In addition, I'm scheduling a dementia test."

"No." The old man glared at the doctor. "My granddaughter's here, she will tell me when I need a test like that."

The doctor focused on his patient. "You don't think you need a dementia test?"

"I read the *Kansas City Star* and the *Kingseater* every day. I study the stock market and watch the news. I read books, I drive, I go to church, I pray. I've never gotten lost. I live right down the street there. I'm goin' fishin'!"

The doctor looked at Kate. "Do you see signs of dementia?"

Kate studied the doctor. "Is there something specific you're looking for, Doctor?"

"I understand your grandfather had a competency case scheduled in court, but it was dropped."

"Who told you that?" Kate stood up and put her hands to her hips. "No, out with it. Who told you my grandfather had a competency case?"

"Never mind, I misspoke. He's ninety-two years old, his insurance will cover it."

"I see no signs of dementia—just stubbornness." She looked at her grandfather. "He lives right down the street. He talked about moving back to Squaw Valley Nursing Home, but he's changed his mind, haven't you?"

The old man looked at Kate and nodded in agreement.

The doctor checked the chart, "I would like to discuss his end-of-life decisions, in case we have an incident like the day before yesterday. Mr. Anderson, do you understand what a medical power of attorney is? Do you understand what a 'Do Not Resuscitate' order is?"

"Yes, and you don't have to talk to me like I'm a retard."

The doctor looked at Kate.

"Not exactly politically correct, but he's right. And we're not deaf!" Kate shouted at the doctor.

He looked down at his patient. "Please explain what your wishes would be if we were to have an incident like yesterday again. Do you want us to resuscitate you? It could be very painful."

"Yes, I want you to do everything in your power to save me. Unless there is no way I will ever get any better—I don't want to live like a vegetable." The old man stuck his tongue out and moved it to the side of his face, threw his head back, rolled his eyes and pretended he was unconscious. And, just as quickly, he opened his large brown eyes and blinked like an owl.

Kate suppressed a giggle.

The doctor glared at Kate. "I expected to get a DNR today, he's ninety-two."

"Are you scolding me, Doctor? You have his paperwork, drawn up by an attorney. We've been over this DNR issue three times now in two days." Kate held up her fingers indicating the number three. Pops did the same. "You heard the man, he wants you to do everything in your power to save him. Besides, you're not his regular doctor. I've never heard anything so outrageous."

"He's refusing tests. He's refusing to sign a DNR. He's going against medical advice. I'm writing him a prescription for Aricept."

"Isn't that a dementia drug? You're not giving him another prescription which may cause side effects—he's on thirteen scripts now."

"You're leaving against doctor's advice." He clicked his pen, pushed it into his pocket protector and strode out the door.

"Hey, hey, let's go home." Pops grinned and raised his arms in a touchdown victory.

"Not so fast, Pops, breakfast is coming. You've been so weak. We should sign their papers, that way we know your diagnosis. I promise we'll go home right after breakfast." Kate picked up his chart and tried to decipher the cryptic notes.

CHAPTER TWENTY

THE CHAMBER

T he Founders met in the basement of the Kingseat bank building. Except for the security system and the keypad in the alleyway, the meeting place had not changed in forty years. The carpet—trodden with paths to the bar, the exit and bathroom—was a mere pad hiding the concrete floor. The walls, now a dirty yellow, highlighted the time when cigars were dispensed like candy, and rings of smoke were blown in the air. Gone were the formalities of the meeting, the secret handshake, and red jackets. The covert meeting took place on Law Day for the Circuit Court. That way, the dates and times were unpredictable, and attorneys were in town for court.

The meeting ran much like a wolfpack. The president, Howard Bone, attorney-at-law, was top dog. His second, the accountant and faithful guard Anthony Asmus, was the enforcer. The two received the most money and made the decisions. The other men in the room had been carefully selected for their use to the society. The two isolated themselves from the rest of the group, always choosing men who did not travel in the same social circles.

Ironically, the president and vice-president worked in the same office building, shared a neighborhood and a church. The pack speculated whether their leaders shared other dirty secrets. There had been rumors about the society over the years, but no one ever cared to investigate.

At age seventy-nine, the attorney knew his days were numbered. The problem—who would succeed him? The accountant and the attorney couldn't stomach any of the other members. The two discussed the accountant taking the president's job, but who would be the vice-president? Certainly not the sergeant-at-arms or the slimy Tanner Tucker, the developer.

Bone raised his glass of whiskey. "Cheers," echoed through the basement. "The November meeting will be called to order."

"Sergeant-at-Arms, have you secured the premises?"

"Yes sir." He glanced over at the screen showing the outside of the building.

Bone continued, "We will start with old business. Any old business? Anything to report?"

The local auctioneer said, "Let the record reflect no old business to report."

The crowd clinked glasses and chuckled with one another.

"All right, all right, settle down. Treasurer, will you read the balance of our account?"

"The ledger reads one million, three hundred thousand dollars. This is the list of the distributions that will be made next month." A single sheet of paper passed hand to hand through the group as each man studied it carefully and passed it on.

"As agreed by all, more of a distribution will be made next month. As you all know, this cash is distributed after the next meeting. As always, the sergeant-at-arms has made arrangements for you to have access to your safety deposit boxes. The jeweler will be on hand if anyone needs to buy something for the wife, or girlfriend."

The crowd laughed and pointed at the doctor, the city councilman and the developer.

"Are you going to show us pics of your girlfriend this month?" a man in the back yelled. The other men laughed and guffawed about the women. Several elbowed each other and sipped their drinks in anticipation.

The accountant, Asmus, yelled, "Come to order, you morons!"

"Please let me continue. I need to get home early this evening," Bone talked barely above an old man's whisper. "Tucker brings a list of properties which he believes the individual group members might be interested in. Our goal is to invest in our future."

"And to launder our dirty money," the auctioneer yelled from the back.

The Sergeant fed the list of distributions through the shredder for dramatic effect. The accountant yelled, "Come to order, remember, none of you get caught depositing too much cash into your personal accounts, keep it under $10,000. If we can't settle down tonight, I will dismiss this meeting." He glared at the auctioneer who seemed to be the rowdiest of the crowd. "All agreed?"

"Agreed," the ten men stated in unison.

The auctioneer raised his hand.

"No, Sam, I didn't forget you—Sam has some nice properties coming up for auction. He also has antiques, jewelry, old coins—all taken from some of our 'special clients'. He has pictures to show you." Sam started passing out flyers.

Bone cut in, "Don't be so needy, Sam, everyone knows how this works."

The accountant stepped up to the podium. "Crap, Howard, move on to new business."

"Next order of business. Anyone on our list die?"

The sergeant-at-arms, in normal life, the banker, answered. "Annie Jones died last week. With no will, her estate is moving through probate and the initial ads in the paper have gone out. It's not a big estate, no executor. The judge assigned it to H.O.G.G."

The auctioneer slapped the judge on the back.

"Any members added to the distribution list besides H.O.G.G. and the judge to Annie Jones?" said Bone.

No one spoke.

"Then, of course, H.O.G.G. receives 20%, the judge receives 20%, and the rest will be divided equally among members at the end of the quarter."

"Anyone following up on the Warren Collins estate?"

A newer member, the younger attorney, Robert Shannon, stated, "Mr. Collins hired an out-of-town law firm. It's gone."

"Moving on, any new prospects?"

This time, the accountant addressed the group. "I would like to submit a name—Helen Doyle. Does anyone have any connections to Mrs. Doyle?"

"You do," a voice came from the back of the room as everyone laughed.

"Yes, I'm aware. Here's your chance to be placed on the list for a larger cut. We need at least two members to add her name to our list. I may not have the best way to approach her."

"I do. I clean her jewelry and go to church with her. I doubt we can get this one, but it's worth a try," said the jeweler. "She's been moved to the nursing home. Let's add her, we can always scratch her off the list."

"Let's move along, no other prospect?" presided Bone.

"How many do we have?" asked the accountant.

"Scratching two off, adding one, that makes nineteen."

"Let's think, gentlemen. We've met our goal, but some of these may not pan out. Be careful. The

Anderson—I mean Freking—estate should be our wake-up call. Now on to the main event of the evening: the lottery."

The auctioneer interrupted. "What do you mean, our 'wake-up call?' Be careful? Is there a problem?"

"A granddaughter has come into the picture. We have it handled. See Tucker or Asmus for details. Let's move on."

"As you know, the Freking estate had three members involved. The attorney, the accountant, the doctor and, of course, our member pot. The auctioneer will conduct the lottery. There are four lots. Lot Number One."

"I thought there were five," the doctor said.

"The attorneys have reviewed the case. Number five, the red barn farm, has been taken out for now. We believe there's a possibility Kate Anderson, the granddaughter, has a claim to that property and we don't want anyone to be involved in a lawsuit, do we, Doctor?" The president paused for dramatic effect and the accountant stared at the doctor.

"If she doesn't proceed, we will give you a chance later. We are watching her movements. Of course, since you are retiring and moving, you will no longer be attending meetings, but you will just have to trust we will be fair with you. Do you have any problem with that, Doctor?"

The doctor hung his head like Tiger Woods after he missed a shot. "No problem."

Bone continued. "Has everyone had the opportunity to review the property and the assessments?"

Drinks went up and everyone said, "Aye."

"Any objections to this auction tonight?"

"Nay." The crowd toasted.

"Auctioneer, would you review the terms?"

The auctioneer came out of the shadows. He was a tall, middle-aged man wearing a cowboy hat and Wrangler jeans. He strode to the front of the room, now all business. "As you all know, you need to bring your paperwork to claim your property. I kept it simple," the auctioneer grinned. "This is your paperwork." He held up four small business cards: one, two, three, four. Don't lose your paperwork. Howard, draw the first number."

The attorney reached into the hat and drew out a business card. "Freking Estate, Number Two" was scrawled in red ink.

"I'll take it," he said. "Fifty acres, grain bins, and I've always wanted a windmill. Maybe I will build a little commune out there. They are making tiny houses in grain bins now."

The crowd laughed.

The accountant stepped up and drew his number. He bragged, "Lot Number Four. I've drawn the most valuable property, again," and took his seat.

"Doctor, that leaves you." The doctor reached into the hat and pulled the card with "Lot Number Three" written on it. "It's the most saleable piece. I'm happy with that."

"Why don't you make a landing strip for your plane?" someone shouted. The men laughed and gulped whiskey from a bottle sent around the room.

"That leaves the sixty-acre property with a small house. If anyone is interested in this property, see the developer and the auctioneer. This group gets first chance, but it is to be purchased at market value. The money we receive will be accumulated into the account, then divided by this group," explained the attorney.

"We regret we are saying goodbye to our doctor, no fanfare or farewell. We are sorry we didn't wrap up the entire estate while you were here, but we will be fair to you. I assume you will keep in touch."

"You're not done with me yet." The doctor, now quite intoxicated, grinned and toasted the group. He knew he would never see any more of the money but was more than happy with the property he received that night.

The sergeant-of-arms glanced at the monitor. "Call to order! We have a visitor." The group stumbled up to the front of the room and the ten men huddled around the screen. Chief Reese Matthews appeared bigger than life as he exited his vehicle, parked very close to the back door. He leaned against the SUV and looked directly at the camera. He then reached into his pocket, pulled out a small pen knife, and began cleaning his fingernails.

The meeting broke into chaos as unidentified voices spoke. "What in the hell is he doing here?"

"I told you not to hire him. Whatta we gonna do?"

"We're not breaking any laws—we'll just leave."

"Don't be stupid, we've all been drinking, and we can't be seen together."

"I'll call my girlfriend Cammie. We can go out the front," the doctor said.

"Shut up and let's think. Someone make a pot of coffee," the attorney demanded.

"This is a disaster," the auctioneer whined.

"Shut up. All of you just shut up!" the accountant yelled.

CHAPTER TWENTY-ONE

GIRLS ONLY

The apartment, decorated in tiny white snowflakes and fairy lights, could have been a scene from a movie. The lights around the windows overlooking Main Street twinkled and blinked as if in time with the music which played through the speaker system. Small tables and chairs with white linen tablecloths were carefully positioned around the room. Silver balloons danced on ribbons and accented the twinkling lights. Tall fluted glasses on sterling silver trays stood ready for bubbly champagne.

The nursing students, Amy and Emily—hired for the Vlogs—wore short French maid outfits. The two looked almost like twins, their make-up expertly drawn to match each other. In contrast, two hunky men wore tight black pants, white cuffed shirts and wide sashes. With Susie as director, they were practicing bowing and carrying trays. "Don't forget to stay in character, you are to be seen and not heard. Listen to conversations. No drinking until the party is over—sorry."

Kate laughed. "I don't think we have to go that far, Di-rec-tor!" She pulled Susie aside, "the point of the party is to have fun. If we get dirt on the attorneys, accountants or other business leaders in town—great. This is about making connections. We don't want the 'young people' talking about the pair of paranoid older ladies living on Main Street."

Susie interrupted Kate. "Don't listen to her," she said loudly to the four standing near the kitchen island. "I don't know why she is in such a good mood today—she's a real bitch of a boss." She took Kate's arm and walked her over to one of the young men. "Kate, do you remember Art Gage from the car dealership? I called him, like you suggested. He'll make a fine butler/chauffeur. He brought his friend, Ken Hopkins, a professional bartender."

"Hello, Ken, welcome to our little team. Hello, Art, nice to see you again. I love the Dodge Charger." Art performed a perfect bow, "My pleasure, milady."

Susie interrupted, "Don't gab about cars during my party tour. C'mon, Kate, let me show you the necklaces and photo collage in the entry way."

The Kingseat High School Class of 2003 had one hundred fifty students. Seventy–eight were girls and fifteen were emailed an invitation to the party. The senior class pictures had been downloaded and printed. A sterling silver necklace with the letter of the woman's initial circled each picture. Above each picture was a cardboard sign printed in calligraphy with their maiden names. A picture collage hung on the wall with Susie added as one of the gals in the high school.

"Now that's funny," Kate said. "We're giving them silver necklaces? Did we increase our budget?"

"Never mind that now, let's continue our tour." A rustic ornate coat hook hung in the hallway along with two large coat stands. In the living room, Susie printed recent pictures from Facebook and placed them in a scattered array inside a glass-topped table. Wine corks and Kate's book were also included in the display.

"And look here," Susie said, pointing to a table where gift bags were arranged on the table. Each bag contained Kate's book, their business cards, and the information to link to the weekly Vlog, as well as little chocolates and small bottles of essential oils and soaps.

"We're in the business to sell books, not give them away."

"Now over here," Susie said, "we've choices of sparkling champagne, raspberry sweet tea, sodas. Second round of drinks includes margaritas, a gin and tonic punch and whiskey sours, plus vodka in various flavors. Here's the food: small sandwiches, vegetable trays in the fridge, with cookies and cupcakes ordered from a local chocolatier."

"This is wonderful, Susie. I'm not even going to ask how much. The sterling silver necklaces were a little over the top, but it's perfect. Are we going into the party business?"

"We could," Susie said, "it was fun! I hope you like some of these women. It's coming out of the advertising budget. Tax deductible, Darling." She waved her arms in the air and then danced ballerina style around the room like a very tall Barbie fairy.

Amy walked over to Kate. "You two make such a cute couple."

Kate burst out laughing. "We're not a couple. We're friends and business partners. But, sometimes she's my wife."

"And, sometimes, you're mine." Susie didn't have to hear the words to know the implication. "You could do worse, Katie dear."

❧   ❧   ❧

Kate dressed in a basic black V-neck cocktail dress, short above the knee. Her black spike heels strapped up her ankle. Her mane of dark hair, curled at the end, was much like the style she wore in high school. She wore her sterling silver "K" necklace and silver bangle bracelets complete the outfit.

Susie wore a designer leopard pattern dress and tall black heels. She dominated the spotlight.

Pops arrived by limousine, Art his gallant chauffer.

"This is my funeral suit," Pops said as he entered the room.

"You're very handsome, Pops." Kate kissed him on the cheek. "Pops, this is Amy—she's your waitress tonight. Anything you need, just wave to her and she'll get it for you. But, let's keep your whiskey to two." Kate held up two fingers, and he nodded his head in agreement, but the look on his face was too innocent.

"Pops, the stairs. We don't want Susie to have to carry you out."

The old man looked at Susie and gave her a little wink. She laughed and gave him a hug. "I would sling you over my shoulder like a sack of potatoes, but I think we could find you a place here."

"No, I'll go home, I have a date with a beautiful nurse who gives me my medicine."

Harriett Quinn and Jennifer Doyle arrived together.

"Welcome and thanks for coming, ladies. I don't believe you've met my business partner, Susie Jones. Susie, this is Harriett. I told you she helped me when Pops was in the Squaw Valley Nursing Home. I was a little stressed that day, Harriett, I hope you didn't think ill of me."

"Oh no, I understand. What a shock for you. And, really, he is settled in a much nicer facility now."

"And, Susie, this is Jennifer Doyle. She works for H.O.G.G."

"Kate, there's a picture of the two of you in one of the Spanish class pictures. Come with me, ladies. I'll show you the pictures, and then we'll get a drink."

Jennifer, dressed in her usual tan colors, tried to blend into the beige wall in the hallway. Kate didn't let her disappear. "Jennifer, did you keep your Spanish up after high school?"

"No, I studied accounting—numbers are more my thing."

"Where did you go to college?"

Jennifer looked down and away, "I graduated from Stephens College in Columbia. It's a small school, you've probably never heard of it."

"Oh, sure, a very good school, Jennifer. Do you miss Columbia, isn't it a hip town?"

"No, I've always been a homebody."

Susie took Harriett and listened to all the farm stories of cats and dogs and their pet racoon. The group settled at a tall table for four overlooking Main Street. Of course, Kate mingled around the room, but Susie stayed with the two, making sure she had every opportunity to talk about gossip in Kingseat.

❧   ❧   ❧

An hour and a half later, Kate looked at the clock and walked over to Pops. "You're getting tired, Pops."

"Yes, Kate, put the old man to bed so this party can get started. I've never been to a girls-only party. It was an honor to be here."

"Girls only, except for you, Pops." Kate gave Pops a hug.

Amy stepped up. "Theodore, would you like for me to ride with you in the limo? I'll walk you in. I think your nurse is expecting you."

"Yes, honey, I'd follow you anywhere." Pops' eyes sparkled as he said his goodbye.

The music cranked up and a new round of drinks and little cucumber sandwiches were passed around the room.

Kate heard the door and saw an unexpected guest arrive. Kate crossed the room in a few seconds, "Welcome, Cammie, I'm glad you decided to pop in."

"I wasn't planning to come but decided I might as well reconnect with old friends."

"Please come in, let me take your coat." Kate said.

Susie danced over to the new guest. "You've arrived just in time, everyone has had a few drinks and is loosening up, we're going to have such fun. We're into the vodka now. Or would you prefer something else?"

"Vodka will be fine. I need a drink."

Art responded, indicating the different flavors of vodka on his tray. The music rocked to the beat of the 90's and Emily served an assortment of small sandwiches and chocolates.

"This is quite the party," Cammie said. "I didn't know what to expect. I thought I was busy tonight, but it appears I've been stood up, again."

"Men—I assume it was a man?" Susie said.

"Susie, did you know Cammie worked at Pops' doctor's office? Pops just left, he would have loved to see you."

"He is such a dear man. How's he doing?"

"He's doing great."

"Boring, boring, Kate, this is a party. Come over to the kitchen island, Cammie, let's trash men. Mine is on his best behavior, but the relationship is new. How long have you been with yours?"

Susie grilled Cammie until she spilled about her doctor-friend who'd been leading her on for the last three years. "He said he loved me, and we would get married."

"Dirty, well, let's see if we can fix this. Kate and I have come up with a few ideas on how to deal with men."

Dancing started after Kate kicked off her shoes and encouraged Amy, Emily, and the rest of the guests to do the same. The ladies rocked to the 90's playlist on the iPod with speakers.

Harriett stopped dancing and said, "I've got to go home. I promised Michael I would be home by midnight."

The speakers came alive with the song, "Run Away." Susie and Kate danced to their own version of the Real McCoys' song. The guests applauded and at the end the two took dramatic bows.

"Someone's been watching way too many YouTube videos," Kate laughed.

Harriett approached the two. "I really have to go— this has been so much fun, thank you for inviting me."

"You're so sweet, it's been fun reconnecting with you, Harriett."

"Kate, could I talk with you a moment in private?"

"Absolutely, let's go out into the hall for a second."

Harriett reached in her pocket and pulled out two square pieces of paper that had been smoothed, but at one time were crumpled.

"Kate, I hope I can trust you. You must understand I could get fired for giving these to you. Your grandfather escaped the nursing home just in time. These medications are for people who are disruptive, agitated or violent—not your grandfather. I don't know why he would have prescribed them. Please, don't tell anyone. Thank goodness Doctor Williams is retiring."

Kate stared at the prescriptions. "Harriett, your secret is safe with me. No amount of coercing would ever get it out of me. I'm so glad you told me. I thought I was just being paranoid. I promise, I will shred these tonight. C'mon, let's get Jennifer and get you home. Promise me you won't worry."

"I promise."

Kate and Harriett hugged in the stairway as Jennifer opened the door with her coat on.

Kate turned and smiled at Jennifer. "Thanks for coming, Jennifer. I hope you had a good time."

"I did. You aren't anything like I expected. You were never mean to me in high school or did anything like that, but I just never liked you."

"Jennifer, in my mind, I was just trying to survive, like many of us were. But, it would be awful to learn that I was a bully."

"I was going to leave this at the party. Don't open it now, but I wanted to hand it to you personally."

Jennifer handed Kate a small envelope. "Don't open it now."

"Are you okay to drive, Harriett? We have a handsome chauffeur." Kate smiled at the two women.

"No, no, I'm fine, I only drank a glass of wine hours ago. Michael wouldn't like it if I were chauffeured home by a man."

Susie joined the women with the gift bags. "Don't forget your little bag. And, if you like the book, please put a positive comment on Amazon."

A line of ladies formed at the door and the waitresses gathered coats.

"No need for you to go, the party will survive midnight, surely some of you can stay past Cinderella's curfew," Susie said.

Art Gage turned the music to more modern tunes and the remaining ladies danced around the room.

CHAPTER TWENTY-TWO

THE HIDE-OUT

S usie Jones stumbled into the living room and surveyed the area. The trash can overflowed with cups, plates, napkins, and beer bottles. The smell of coffee floated in the air and Susie walked straight for the pot. She sat at one of the party tables and watched the cars go by on Main Street. *A beautiful little town with an underbelly of evil.*

Kate strode through the doorway, fully dressed in jeans, a sweatshirt and work boots. "Wow, this place is a mess. I can't believe we went to bed without cleaning up a thing."

"Why did we schedule the trip to the cabin this morning?" Susie sipped her coffee and grimaced.

"We had a little delay with Pop's hospital stay, remember? I can't wait to see it and I've a crew lined up today."

"Shh…my head—let them sleep." Susie motioned to their friends, Amy and Emily, lying like bookends on the couch.

"Okay, no problem. Drink your coffee." Kate poured herself a cup and smelled the fragrant aroma of Hazelnut.

"Would you be a love and run down to the diner and pick up breakfast?"

"Sure, what do you think they'll want?"

"Order a little of everything. And, Kate—don't hurry. I'll need some time. On second thought—no eggs."

"Did you read the note from Jennifer?"

"Oh yes! Oh—my head. Wow, this is big, isn't it?"

"It helps, not proof of anything, but we may have a whistleblower or at least a witness. It might be enough to get a criminal investigation open. I see your eyes glazing over. Drink your coffee, we'll talk later."

∽ ∽ ∽

Kate walked around the corner to the Mug Shot Diner. She noticed the table of older men sitting in the middle of the room and recognized Tucker, the appraiser of the farms. Tucker billed thirty-six hundred dollars for an appraisal on each of the five farms. Kate had been sent an e-file—not even a hard copy. She glared at Tucker and slid onto a stool next to Clayton Clark.

"Good morning, it was nice to visit with your wife last night. She's the real deal, isn't she?"

"I'm a lucky man. Where's your friend?"

"She got rid of me, so she could mix some Bloody Mary's. Two ladies stayed, and I think they were up all night."

"So, what's the plan, are you going with us?" Clayton asked.

"If you don't mind, start without me. The cabin has been vacant about ten months—I just now got possession of it. Can you take pictures? The trustee couldn't find the keys. You may have to break in."

"Not a problem, we can get in."

"A man of few words, I like it. I'll bring ice and cold drinks and we'll run and get anything you need. You brought a rifle?"

"Yes, ma'am, and a shotgun."

"Let me buy you and the crew breakfast."

"You don't need to do that."

"I know." Kate turned on the stool, looking at the patrons in the restaurant.

"Okay, but the boys order the special—biscuits and gravy, two orders. I'll get mine."

"Don't be silly, I'm buying for everybody at the apartment, and breakfast meals are cheap. It makes me look like a nice lady."

"Somethin' I should tell you—we're related. I'm your second cousin. My maternal grandmother was born an Anderson. Most of the Andersons around here are related one way or the other."

"What? Pops said he didn't have any family here."

"Well, I suppose that's how they dealt with it—big feud years ago. The younger generations don't care

159

about what happened. I've downloaded the whole family tree, I can even bring it up on my phone. See." He held up his phone and swiped over to her grandfather's line. "Interesting fact, your great, great grand-pappy came over from Sweden and bought forty acres not far from your grandfather's place. It's an interesting story."

"Wow. I'm speechless. Thanks for telling me. Can you send the tree to my email?"

"Sure thing. They're some good people in this town. They see what goes on. Kate, you're not alone."

∽   ∽   ∽

The soy beans yellowed in the fields, bursting at the seams. Susie drove Kate's Dodge Charger through the unlocked gate and pulled around the ten-acre lake choked with algae and lily pads from neglect. It stood out like a swamp against an otherwise picturesque setting. The trees turned shades of orange and lined the driveway at the back of the yard. Large fist-sized green walnuts fell as squirrels raced to bury their stash for winter.

"Wow, this place brings back memories. It was always so peaceful pulling through the gate—like unlocking a secret, special world. We left all our troubles behind," Susie said.

"When I was about five, Pops threw me off the dock and told me to swim. He watched too many John Wayne movies. It was a good thing I could wade out."

Two pickups and a large black trailer were pulled in close to the cabin. A young man stood near one of the trucks. He vomited up his breakfast.

"Oh my God, do you think it's that bad? I'm not feeling so great—I'm staying out by the lake, even though—what a nasty mess. What's in the lake?"

"Pull around to the front deck." Kate pointed for Susie to pull into the yard. "The lake hasn't been treated this year. It will take work to get it clean again."

"This is truly heartbreaking. Your grandparents kept this place immaculate."

"It is what it is," Kate said.

Clayton met her at the sliding glass door of the deck, picked up a chair, and turned it over. "Have a seat—I think you better sit down."

"I'm fine. Is he okay?" Kate motioned to a young man pacing back and forth behind the cabin.

"Yeah," Clayton chuckled. "I think he might have partied last night. He usually has a pretty strong stomach, but the stench is bad. Do you want the good news or the bad news?"

"I'm going down to the lake, give me the camera." Kate handed Susie the camera and snapped a quick pic of Kate and Clayton. They ignored her.

"Good news."

"The structure itself is good, it's made like a little bomb shelter. The bad news is—I'd like to set a bomb off inside. You might be able to save the refrigerator." Clayton looked down at his feet.

"The refrigerator? Seriously, that's it?"

"The air conditioner came on and it's blowing putrid air. We're running it full blast. We'll check the heat soon."

"We'll need a fridge and heat—hopefully it will work. But I'm guessing I'll need new beds," Kate said.

"Oh yeah. Everything else—it's broken or has mold growing on it. Dishes, pots, and pans might be able to be washed up. But you've got dead mice and poison pellets everywhere. We shot a squirrel eating his way through the plywood covering the crawl space. We got here in the nick of time—you'd have had a total loss if the squirrel had made his way in. They'll gnaw through everything including your wiring."

"Well then, we saved the day." Kate threw up her hands in victory.

"We also killed a black snake—but don't tell your granddad. It measured about seven-foot long and I bet he's been here for years. They're treasured in Missouri for their voracious appetite for mice, but you don't want him in the house. Sam tried to corral him in a bucket, and the snake struck at him." Clayton laughed.

"We called him Blackie. He lived in the shed out by the burn barrel. Pops would order me to run out to get his fishing pole and then he would yell, 'watch out for Blackie' and laugh. I'm not sad he's gone. Where there is one, there are two. Try to catch the next one. We usually use the rake. I have a place for him."

Clayton laughed. "Remind me not to get on your bad side."

A piercing scream echoed from the lake. Susie ran up the dock ramp and into the yard. Her blonde hair flew in the wind and the camera bounced around her neck. Her long legs high stepped in her tall boots. "Eww. Eww."

"Oh no," Kate said.

"Uhh—we threw the snake into the lake—turtle food."

"It's okay, Susie. I'll take you back to town."

"The hell you say. And miss all the excitement? I was startled. It's fine. Big snake–that was a *very* big snake. Let's get to work."

"Okay, gloves and paper masks. Be careful where you step. First on the list, I'm looking for two shot guns and a rifle."

"They're gone," Clayton said. "It looks like teenagers lived here."

Kate walked into the kitchen. Dirty dishes were smashed on the floor and the porcelain oven top was broken to pieces. She turned on her heels, "Someone took a ball bat to the kitchen."

She strode into the living room where the sofa was riddled with holes. Pop's recliner lay in pieces on the floor. "They stole the TV, radio, and a couple of lamps." Kate wandered into the bedroom where mold crawled up the wall. The once carefully made bed was a

163

rumpled mess on the floor. The curtains were shredded as if some wild cat had been set loose inside.

"These weren't teenagers, this is the work of the farmhands. Dumb asses. The same guys Pops gave Christmas bonuses to every year and bought them supper once a month. It pisses me off, but let's get to work. Take everything out. We might try to save some quilts. Grandma Helen made them. Open all the unbroken windows."

"You heard the lady, take everything out."

"Clayton, why don't we walk down by the lake and look at it. We may need more than just your guys. What's the best way to get rid of moss?"

"It's late in the year, but I know a guy who rakes his out with wire fencing. Do you want me to call him?"

"Yes, please, and check out the dock to make sure it is stable. We want to get Pops out there as soon as possible. The weather is supposed to be beautiful a couple of days next week. How 'bout somebody who can mow this yard?"

"Yes, ma'am. I know a young woman who lives in town. She'll mow later this evening."

"Our main goal is to get Pops fishin'."

"They might have fished you out."

Kate blushed. "They better not have fished us out—that's all I've got to say."

A white Chevy Malibu pulled into the drive and slowly made its way around the curve.

"Oh crap, here comes Pops. This is liable to kill him."

"Let me talk to him, Kate, sometimes bad news is better man to man. I'll keep him out of the house. He knows me from church. I'll talk to him about fishing next week."

CHAPTER TWENTY-THREE

IN THE NAME OF THE FATHER

E very candle in the newly restored church was lit. Eerie shadows danced against the walls and the smell of Frankincense filled the air. Antique statues, once worn and dull, sparkled with new paint. The entire ceiling and walls were patched and re-patched, then painted in soft hues of pink and yellow. The pews were polished with new varnish. The priest flung the smoky incense over the coffin. The chain groaned and squeaked as the ancient censor was flung in the air.

Kate Anderson stood tall and straight in the front pew, her eyes fixed on Saint Francis, the one saint she could rely on. She wore a small black pillbox hat with a veil, and a grey dress with a matching coat. Susie stood on one side and Will Johnson stood on the other. She could feel Reese Matthews' shadowy presence at her back. She fought back tears and memories as the priest in the white robe and gold stole began the prayer. "In the name of the Father, the Son and the Holy Spirit."

The memory of the telephone call replayed in Kate's brain. "I'm sorry, Kate, your grandfather has passed. He got out of bed and, well, we found him on the floor, almost in the hall."

She shook her head, fighting the memory. Will reached down and took her hand. He put her gloved hand to his lips and kissed it. She laced her fingers into his.

Susie whispered in Kate's ear, "Look at all the flowers, your granddad would be very proud." Kate let go of Will's hand and hugged her friend. A public show of affection unheard of in her family, Kate grabbed onto her new life.

"He would be more pleased if the money had gone to the school."

She drifted off into her own thoughts about the Sisters of Saint Francis who taught her when she was in school. *It was so nice of them to drive over. I think there are only seven still at the abbey, a dying vocation and way of life.*

The crowd stood for the gospel reading of the day. A young visiting priest, in his early twenties, struggled to climb the pulpit stairs. His legs were twisted, and his left arm fell unused at his side. He transformed when he read the word of God, and his voice rang out like music in the church. When he finished, he kissed the Bible and returned to his body that betrayed him. The priest stepped into the pulpit and everyone sat. Father Holloway spoke about love and peace and avoided looking at Kate, his eyes fixed somewhere in the choir.

Not one word was spoken for or about Theodore Anderson, deceased.

Will, Kate, and Susie sat in the front pew and watched the communion procession. Kate continued to stare at her favorite saint. Some people came by and shook Kate's hand. Diana Birdsell, Pops' friend from the restaurant, declined communion, went straight for Kate, and the two women hugged. The communion procession became a receiving line, and the three stood up as people ignored the priest and spoke to Kate.

One man who looked like a younger version of Pops said, "I'm your grandfather's first cousin, Jim." Then another cousin came by, and then another until Kate could not remember all the names. Clayton Clark came and shook Kate's hand, and his wife gave her a quick hug.

The priest finished communion and stood behind the altar. The crowd finished their procession back to their pews.

Susie leaned over and whispered to Kate, "The priest—he looks like he's sixteen years old."

"I know—but somehow he secured a fifty-seven-thousand-dollar donation from Pops for the church's restoration. He tithed till the end." Kate shook her head and then grinned.

The soloist sang *Amazing Grace*. Kate hummed with the music. Susie soon joined in, and then Will joined her in song. Their beautiful voices formed a serenade, almost an echo. Tears welled in Kate's eyes and ran down her cheeks. She was not the only one moved by the beautiful song. A woman blew her nose like a fog horn and Kate laughed, a young girl's laughter, a giggle she had not heard since she was a young girl sitting in this same pew.

The priest took center stage again and raised both arms in praise.

Eternal Rest,
Grant unto them O Lord
And let perpetual light
Shine upon them,
May their souls
And the souls
Of the faithful departed
Rest in Peace.

The crowd replied, "Rest in Peace."

Kate stated "Amen." The crowd echoed "Amen." She wiped her tears with her grandmother's handkerchief and stood tall. Her little pillbox hat never moved on top of her head as she exited the church, eyes straight ahead. Hours of practice walking with books on her head paid off today.

She walked to the waiting limo. Will waved the chauffer away and opened the door for her. She stepped in, and Susie and Will climbed in after her. Kate watched in silence as the crowd exited the church. The car moved away from the curb. "Stop," Kate yelled from the back seat. The driver obeyed, and the three passengers jolted forward with the sudden halt. Kate pushed the button, and the window lowered. Reese Matthews walked up to the limousine. "Get in," Kate said.

The large man removed his white hat, climbed into the limo, sat next to Susie, and took her hand. Susie sobbed against his shoulder. Kate could see the crowd whispering in the background. The limo moved on.

"That should give the gossips something to talk about," Kate said.

Reese looked at Kate, "It was a beautiful service. I almost cried during *Amazing Grace*."

"I just realized my biological grandmother died on the same day, twenty-seven years apart."

Susie looked up and dabbed her eyes. "Wow, Kate, that's a little eerie." She then pulled out her compact and checked her make-up.

"It's synchronicity. Almost like—everything now has clicked into place. Where before—it was just a chaotic, random mess."

"And tomorrow's Thanksgiving. Please come over, we've enough food to feed an army and I'm sure cousins will bring more tonight. I bet we'll have pie." Kate smiled through her tears.

CHAPTER TWENTY-FOUR

YOU'VE BEEN MADE

Reese Matthews stood near his city-issued SUV in the parking lot outside the Kingseat Bank. A patient man, he wanted to be up close when the men came out of the building. More out of boredom than confirmation, he ran all plates on the cars parked in the lot. He knew who would be coming out. Some men he had never met; he planned to meet them tonight. He checked his list with the list from Jennifer's note from the party and they all matched. A cold night, but that didn't bother the chief.

Wow, she looked great tonight. She is totally out of my league. Susie Jones, what do I know about you?

Steve Blakely, Matthews' assistant, had been given the assignment of running a background check on Susie Jones, Kate Anderson's best friend.

What's taking him so long—this should've been routine.

The radio crackled, "201 what's your twenty, sir?"

"Call me on my cell, 204." The chief never wanted to give his location over the radio—too many nosy citizens listened to their police scanners. For Matthews, it was a safety issue as well as a personal issue, a procedure he wanted to review in his new small-town police department.

The chief's phone rang, and Blakely spoke. "Sir, I would like to deliver this information to you personally."

"I'm parked in the lot behind the State Bank."

"Yes sir."

"Drive around the block first. I'm checking to see if there are men leaving the front of the bank building. If there are, park and say 'affirmative' over the radio."

"Yes sir."

"Take your time, Blakely."

❧   ❧   ❧

Steve Blakely drove around the square but did not see anyone. At 7:30 p.m. on a Monday night, most vehicles were off the street. Lights were on in the photography store, nothing unusual. He made a larger loop encompassing sixteen blocks and also drove down by the local bar. The lights were on, country music blared, but he didn't see anyone on the street. He drove around the back of the square near the police station and parked next to the chief.

"Good evening, Blakely. You've received information you couldn't share over the phone?" The chief stood outside Blakely's car with his left hand on top of the police car.

"Yes sir, I ran the background on Susie Jones, but please don't think I'm joking."

The chief chuckled, "Blakely, I can't recall one of your jokes—why would I think that?"

"Sir, is there something I should know—about the bank? You're not on a stakeout, are you?"

"There's no robbery in progress if that's what you mean."

"No sir—well, yes sir, that's what I meant. I've got your report—but don't kill the messenger."

"Go on, Blakely, I'm not a grizzly bear.

"Well, sir, here goes. Susie Jones legally changed her name. I was able to follow her trail. Thirteen years ago, she turned up at the Southeast Missouri State College in Springfield, Missouri, as a freshman with a full-ride scholarship. Now sir, it's not fraud, or anything illegal. She applied as an independent student under a legal name."

"Who was she before that?"

"Sir, her name is Katherine Winston of the New England Chocolate Company. They sell chocolates all over the world. Sir, here's her picture. She's a brunette!"

The chief stared at Blakely and grabbed the documentation. He placed the file on top of the car and shuffled through the file. He lingered over a newspaper article which featured Susie playing on the golf team.

"Blakely, are her parents alive, have they been looking for her?"

"Yes, sir. They're alive, and they looked for her for about two years. News channels in New Jersey covered the story of the missing girl, and they ran ads in the paper. It appears she ran away."

"How can this be?"

"I don't know sir, it was an easy trail to follow. Any detective or adequate private investigator could have done it. Susie, um, Katherine was a golf prodigy, probably could have gone professional. I suppose having wealthy parents looking for you nixed that plan. It looks like she cut all ties with her family. But, I don't have the full story."

"Blakely, we're gonna switch vehicles for a short time. Sit in my vehicle and watch this back door." He removed his white Stetson and placed it on Blakely's head. It slid down Blakely's face, but he pushed it to the back of his head where it balanced precariously. "Act like you're me, sit up tall."

"Sir, there are procedures we should follow if we exchange vehicles."

"You're right, Blakely, I'll walk. You okay to sit in my vehicle?"

"Well, yes sir, if you say so, sir."

"Lock your car. Write down my mileage and if you're called to an emergency, swing by Susie Jones' apartment and pick me up. You're not on active duty, is that correct? Here are my keys."

"Yes sir."

Reese walked two blocks to the apartment. He climbed the stairs two at a time and knocked on the apartment door. Susie answered the door in a white fluffy bathrobe, a pink silk nightgown showing underneath. She was in the process of a pedicure, with cotton balls squished out between her toes.

"Come in, Reese, what are you doing here? It's freezing out there. Where's your signature hat?"

Reese stepped through the doorway. Soft music played in the background and twinkly lights decorated all the windows. Kate was sitting at the bar in a sweatshirt and jeans, her long legs wrapped around the barstool legs. She looked up from her laptop, nodded to him. "What's he doing here?"

"Be nice, Kate. We never get visitors, let alone hunky ones. Catching me unexpected, barely dressed." She caressed Reese's chest.

"We need to talk, Susie."

"I'm the winner! Winner, winner chicken dinner." Kate spun around on the bar stool and grinned at Reese. "You get to buy us dinner."

Reese glared at Kate.

"Reese Matthews, have you been checking up on me?"

Reese looked at Susie. "I'm not sure what to call you—Susie, Katherine or your stage name. Did you two place a bet on when I would run a background?"

"We did—and Kate won. I'll never get used to the idea that my best friend knows my boyfriend better than I do."

"I'm your boyfriend? Since when?"

"Since two days ago, when Kate and I made the bet."

"Sounds about right to me," Reese grinned. "And, she doesn't know near what you know about me."

"Eww - TMI. Too much information," Kate yelled from the bar. "Are we going out to dinner or what?"

"Did you forget my stakeout, friend of my girlfriend?"

"Nope, but you're leaving, she's got to get ready, and I'm hungry. I'll bet the rats will leave the bank before nine o'clock. We can still make the diner. I'll call and let them know to save us three chicken dinners."

"All right then. I'll walk back and shake some hands. How long have you known, Kate?"

"From the beginning," Susie said. "I'm a Katherine, who goes by the name of Susie, she's a Kathleen who goes by the name of Katrina or Kate. It was just one of those weird coincidences that bond people together."

"We also bonded over a Runaway song—she ran away from her folks, and eventually I ran away from the law. The only fight we ever had was over you. That one is settled for good. Her family is way more messed up than mine. You two should talk about it some time, but not tonight. I'm hungry," Kate said.

❧   ❧   ❧

Reese Matthews walked in front of the bank, lost in thought about the two women and their connection. He was so preoccupied, he almost ran into the accountant and attorney walking out the front door of the bank.

Matthews caught himself, "Good evening gentlemen, meeting at the bank tonight?"

"No, what makes you think there was a meeting tonight?"

"All the cars parked out back."

"What are you even doing here? How did you get here?"

"It's my job to protect Kingseat citizens and the businesses—especially the bank."

"Well, this isn't any of your concern, is it, Howard?"

"None of your concern, Chief."

"You two aren't planning to drive, are you? You smell like a coffee-whiskey still."

"Again, none of your business, Chief."

"Again, kinda is my business. Do you need a ride home? I can arrange a ride."

"No," the attorney and accountant spoke in unison.

"Have a good evening, gentlemen."

The chief walked around the back of the bank and saw Blakely sitting in the SUV with Reese's white Stetson secured squarely on his head. He chuckled as the jeweler and the auctioneer came out the back door and looked at the SUV. The two were mumbling something about "they thought he had left" when the chief came up behind them.

"Good evening, gentlemen, how are you this evening? Meeting in the bank tonight?"

"Ugh, err, no, sir, not really."

177

"I don't believe we've met," Reese said to the auctioneer. "Of course, I know the councilman."

"Hello, there Chief." The auctioneer with the big hat shook the Chief's hand. "We were walking over to the jewelry store. I need to buy something for my wife for Christmas. We're calling for rides home."

"I'm glad to hear that. You got a poker game goin' on in there, fellas? I play poker."

"No. Ugh… just some city planning stuff."

Blakely exited the Chief's car, removed the Chief's hat and walked towards the three men.

"I wasn't aware the city had approved any overtime, Chief," the city councilman/jeweler dared to question as he looked at Blakely.

"No worries, Councilman, I'm salaried and Blakely is working comp time. He needs a day off at the end of the month and doesn't have any time. I'm an understanding boss, don't you know?"

"We'll be on our way."

"Sounds like a good idea to me," the chief said.

The two men walked down the alley. Blakely turned to the chief.

"Wave to the camera, Blakely, if my calculations are correct, there are six men watching us right now."

CHAPTER TWENTY-FIVE

TWIN DOLLIES

The Methodist Church sat at the edge of the park. Built in mid-century, it was considered one of the few modern buildings in Kingseat, Missouri. The building overlooked the winding river and now the sun was setting over the water. Kate knew the church because she attended Girl Scouts in one of the meeting rooms, the one activity she was allowed to attend as a young girl.

Kate and Susie stood in the windbreak of the church. "Give it a couple of minutes, Kate. We want to be fashionably late," Susie said.

Kate examined Susie. "You look exactly like Dolly Parton, super-sized. You aren't nervous?"

"Of course not. I'm a professional Dolly impersonator. You look great too, and I love the new lacy insert. I'm so proud of the fact you are wearing your bustier. You've got some big knockers, girlfriend. And, you're fantastic as my twin Dolly. No one will recognize you. Have some fun, Kate." Susie jabbed her friend in the ribs with her elbow.

"I feel ridiculous. I'm also a little worried about offending God. I don't want to be struck by lightning."

"Remember the putrid smell of the cabin? This accountant—this low-life in a black suit—will be tasting a bit of girl power. He got paid sixty-two thousand dollars to manage your grandmother's trust. What did Pops get? An early grave." Susie straightened her wig and flipped the long curly edges to the front of her face. She puckered her red lips and took one last glance at her reflection in the hallway mirror.

"Okay, okay. The private investigator reported Anthony is easily embarrassed—let's see if we can embarrass him."

The service began with announcements. A large woman in a flowery dress and ratted hairstyle spoke with a southern twang. "Don't forget the chili supper tomorrow night starting at five o'clock. The proceeds will be used for the new speaker system in the church. We could still use some pies for the dinner. Sign-up sheets are in the back of the church."

"We all are asked to pray for Rebecca Sims who has been admitted to the hospital."

Susie led the way into the rear of the church, Kate tailing her as if they were attached. The twin Dollies first stopped and whispered with the usher inside the door—Susie speaking, Kate echoing her speech. Susie clutched the church booklet and wrapped the usher's arm into hers.

"Find us a seat, kind sir." She turned to Kate, "Come on sister, let's go."

The usher's mouth fell open as he stared at Susie. She prodded him forward, talking and giggling as she strutted down the aisle. He searched the pews, trying to find a safe place to park the two women. Kate followed, taking very short steps down the aisle, swinging her butt and her purse in unison, mimicking Susie.

The middle-aged woman making announcements stopped speaking. The crowd turned when they heard the musical voice coming from behind them. All eyes turned to Susie and Kate. No one seemed ready to share their pew. An older gentleman dressed in a suit and tie moved over. The two women sidestepped into the pew and sat down.

Susie sang out, "Oh, isn't it a beautiful day, and what a beautiful church, I just love this little town, don't you *love* this little ole town?"

Kate put her finger to her lips, "Shh! Please be quiet."

The minister stepped up to the podium. He stared at the women who had entered the church, unable to stop himself from gawking. "Let's begin in song. Please turn to Number 394 in your hymnal, *Come Walk with Me*."

Susie sang above the crowd in her beautiful southern Dolly Parton impersonation. Kate hummed a few words and then sang off key. The congregation turned to look at the two Dollies.

The reverend, a small middle-aged man with a bad comb-over and ill-fitting suit, attempted to regain control of the service. "Any other announcements this

181

evening?" The crowd turned toward the reverend but began whispering again. He looked out into the congregation, "All right, would anyone like to introduce guests this evening?"

A young couple with two toddlers stood up and introduced her mother, Mrs. Laura Cooper, visiting from Iowa City, Iowa.

A tall younger man, mid-thirties, with dark curly hair stood up. "This is Jonathon Smith, he's home on leave." The crowd murmured, "Thank you for your service."

The minister looked over the crowd and glanced at the blonde newcomers.

Susie stood up and waved. Her large bosoms danced. "Anthony, Anthony darling, we're here. Aren't you going to introduce us?"

Everyone in the church turned around, including Anthony Asmus.

"Anthony sweetheart, it's your Dollies, don't you recognize us?"

Anthony Asmus' wife looked at him, "Anthony, do you know those women? She looks like she's speaking to you."

"Of course not," he growled.

"Aw, c'mon sweetie, it's okay. You know you love us." Susie turned to Kate. "He's really been so kind and good to us, hasn't he, Sis?"

Kate nodded her head in agreement. The two women smiled and waved at Anthony. A loud parrot-like voice erupted from Kate. "Yes, he has. He's really been good to us."

Susie took the cue and elaborated. "He's funded our career in Branson, and he sees us every chance he gets. He always writes us a nice check from some place called, H-O-G-G. Hog, isn't that funny? What a name for an accounting firm."

The two giggled and repeated the word, "hog." "He invited us to church, tonight, don't ya see us, Anthony?"

Anthony looked at the minister. "You blasted idiot, call the sheriff."

"Oh, don't be like that, baby, we didn't mean to embarrass you. You know fans like to get our autographs. We thought you would love to see us." Susie turned and looked around for an audience. "Would you all like our autographs?" Women started searching their purses and pulling out pens and paper.

The minister stepped out of the podium and walked toward the women.

Susie said, "Perhaps we should go, Sis. We can meet him in Branson. I told you this wasn't a good idea."

"You told *me*? I told *you*," Kate argued in her high-pitched parrot voice.

Susie edged out of her pew. Suddenly, she jumped up and down and danced a little boob jiggle in her high strappy heels and low-cut silver blouse. She squealed with delight, "Reverend Mike, I'm so happy to meet you. We've heard so much about you. Would you like me to sing a song for y'all?"

183

She clasped her hands in front of her chest. "I love the words to *Rock of Ages* and *Amazing Grace* and many other hymns. People pay good money to come see us." She motioned towards Kate, "Well, not her—but me. She does my errands and hums on stage for a good laugh. You like a good laugh, don't you, Reverend Mike?"

Susie hugged Reverend Mike, rocked him back and forth, and laughed musically. With his short frame and her high heels, she smothered his face with her bosom. His face turned different shades of crimson and she finally let him go.

"Perhaps it would be a good idea if you left. It looks like you're making some people uncomfortable," he stammered.

"Li'l ole me, making people uncomfortable? Oh, Reverend Mike, that's not possible."

Susie stepped around the minister and waved at Anthony Asmus. He sat in the front row of the church. She danced towards him, leading with her ample chest which jiggled with every step.

Anthony stood up and searched the crowd for some ally. Finding no one to help, he side-stepped out of the pew and ran toward the door.

Art Gage stepped out of the shadows in the front of the church, video camera in hand. He captured Anthony's face and his rapid departure from the church. In the background a giggly, jiggly Dolly followed down the aisle.

Susie spun around after Anthony exited the church. "Well, I never. Sister, let's go!"

Kate shook hands with Reverend Mike. "My name is Kate Anderson."

The two ladies broke out into a familiar Dolly Parton song, Susie an almost exact match for Dolly Parton, Kate singing off key. When they reached the back of the church, Kate pulled off her blonde wig and announced in a loud voice, "Y'all might want to check YouTube tonight under the call word H-O-G-G." She turned and sprinted out of the church.

CHAPTER TWENTY-SIX

THE COP STOP

Most days, Kate carried a custom-made Billy club—today disguised as a cane—but it could also transform into an umbrella. The telescoping baton, made with a carbon steel shaft and an aluminum handle, was then covered in an Italian leather. It fit perfectly in her hand. It came equipped with a push button lever to extend, for theatrical effect, and a voice-activated recorder.

Kate walked out of her room, jiving like a teenager. She wore a green hoodie, red ball cap, and big wide dark sunglasses. Her long brown hair was stuffed up into a blonde pixie wig. Faded, sagging jeans with frayed holes and Converse tennis shoes completed her disguise.

Susie laughed. "You look pretty authentic to me. Walk back so I can see your briefs."

Kate obliged.

Susie continued her examination. "Your swagger— too gangsta for this little town. And one more thing, let's lighten your face a bit, or, I know—maybe you should ride a skateboard."

"Stop it, I'm fine. A skateboard is one more thing I'd have to ditch. I've been jogging the route every morning, and I can still sprint. There are lots of hiding places and I'll slip into the coffee shop and join you. It's a misdemeanor worst case scenario."

"So, tell me again, you're ditching the sweatshirt and baseball cap in the Salvation Army donation box. I need to learn this espionage stuff."

"Hardly espionage. Prank, it's just a prank, Susie. Now that I've been seen in public in my yoga pants, I'll slide my jeans and sweat shirt off and dump them in the charity box. I'll keep the wig, it's my favorite boy hair. If someone sees me breaking out the taillight, they will give the description of a teenage boy with a red ball cap and green sweatshirt.

"Are you sure eleven-thirty is the best time?"

"It's the only time. The cops will be focused on lunch. The attorney only works until noon. I can't get into in his garage. Tonight is his church night. Hopefully, he'll get stopped for the broken taillight. "

"Okay, let me see how fast you can shimmy out of those pants, sweatshirt and hat."

"Don't worry, I can get out of my pants. I don't need a mum. One more run through, about your part. You go to the coffee shop and order us salads—something yummy. Take your time looking over the menu."

"If I'm asked, 'Where's Kate? ' I'll say she's running late as usual."

"Susie, if I do get caught, it's just vandalism. I have cash stuck in my bra for bail. And, if I don't show up for lunch, you'll know I'm at the cop shop."

❧   ❧   ❧

That evening the attorney, Howard Bone, and his wife, Melony, drove to church, taking his normal route through the park. Preparations for the Christmas displays were under way and the Parks Department trucks were loading their trucks to end the day at seven o'clock. The attorney saw an officer in a blue uniform motion him to the side of the road. Howard pulled his Cadillac over, put the car in park, and placed his hands on the steering wheel.

The officer approached the vehicle. "Good evening sir, my name is Officer Johnson with the Kingseat Police Department.

"My name is Howard Bone and I am a prominent attorney in this town. My wife and I are on the way to church—we don't want to be late."

"Yes sir, we're conducting safety stops tonight, can I get your license and registration?"

"Oh, for God's sake, I told you who I am, do you think I would go driving around without proper registration?"

"No sir, I don't, but I have been ordered to stop everyone driving through the park this evening."

"I am a licensed weapons carrier. My gun is in the glove box with my registration. My license is in my wallet."

"Let's take this slow, Mr. Bone. Ma'am, would you exit the vehicle and step out with Officer Blakely over there? He will retrieve the registration from your glove box."

Officer Blakely held the door while she exited the vehicle. He opened the glove compartment and retrieved the loaded Glock, then unloaded the weapon and placed it back into the glove box. He quickly found the registration papers and strode to the back of the car.

Bone unbuckled his seatbelt and fumbled for his wallet. "You forgot to ask me for my insurance card."

"I was getting to that, sir." Officer Johnson checked the documents and handed them back to Bone. "They appear to be in order."

"Of course, they're in order. Melony, get back in the car, I hate to be late."

Officer Blakely stood at the back of the car and then spoke to the driver. "It looks like you have a taillight out. If you would pop the trunk, maybe I can fix it."

"What? A broken taillight? Well, I suppose it's possible." Howard popped the trunk.

"The outside shell of your light is shattered, but maybe the bulb will still work." The trunk of the Cadillac eased open. "Gun!" Officer Blakely yelled.

"Mr. Bone, remain seated with your hands on the wheel." Johnson commanded.

Bone placed his hands on the wheel. "That's not my gun. Someone must have put it there."

"Well, sir, we may have a problem. The gun is in plain view in your trunk—are you sure it's not yours?"

"No, it's not mine—damn …" The attorney stopped midsentence. "I want a lawyer, I want a lawyer, do you hear me? I want my son. I'm not answering anymore of your questions."

"Yes, sir, I understand, but please listen carefully. We have a procedure we follow. We will follow that procedure to the letter," Blakely said.

Melony asked, "Why are you harassing us?"

Officer Johnson stepped in, "Ma'am, do you have a gun in your purse?"

Melony started to cry. "No."

"This is your husband, and, is this his car?"

"Yes." Melony composed herself. "I would like to call someone to take me home. My son is an attorney— he will come get me. It's not my car, it's in his name only. I know my rights."

"Ma'am, do you know anything about the gun in the trunk?"

"No, honestly Officer, we were just going to church, can't you let us leave?" Melony started to cry again. "We don't know anything about that gun. He can just let you have it, can't he?" Melony sobbed and her slight frame shook as she cried.

"Oh, shut up, Melony," the attorney barked from the front seat of the car.

A large black SUV circled the curve in the park. The Chief of Police, Reese Matthews, exited his vehicle and strode over.

"Jones—I mean—Johnson, take Mrs. Bone home, I'll assist Blakely here."

Bone yelled, "What in the hell are you doing here? I don't want you here."

"Not very neighborly of you, Mr. Bone." The chief walked back to the trunk. "Blakely, you'd better radio the sheriff, he'll want to be in on this. It looks like the gun that's missing in the Robert O'Dell murder investigation."

CHAPTER TWENTY-SEVEN

TUCKER SPECIAL

T ucker Tanner stood at the kitchen island, looked out his sliding glass doors and viewed the perfectly manicured lawn. His wife was out for the evening at one of her social clubs—Jolly Janes, Purple Hat, PEO, he didn't give a flip. Instead of a hot dinner, he found a bowl, a spoon, and a box of cereal.

"Damn—cereal again. At least, I don't have to listen to her noise—blasted woman," he mumbled to himself. The couple's most recent argument had been about the new Ford 250 diesel truck he bought when he received his share of the money from the Helen Freking estate. She said she thought the truck was "plumb stupid."

He marveled about how many times he got paid from the Helen Freking Trust, as his wife mourned her good friend, Helen. Ellen, Tanner's wife, and Helen grew up together in the small community and rode the same school bus. Helen came up with the idea that they should grow up and marry men who wore ties. Helen would say, "Don't go for any farmer boys or none of them boys who wears suspenders."

Tanner doubled his usual appraisal rate for the five farms involved in the estate—it came to over twenty thousand dollars—then found a professional baseball player for a buyer. The entire package brought four million dollars, almost twice the price of anyone local paying for smaller farms. Tanner had been able to pocket the difference, thus cheating his Founder brothers out of their fair share of the profit. Then, the baseball tickets he was able to get out of the player sweetened the deal. *My, oh my, did I make out like a lucky bastard.*

Tanner grabbed the remote and turned on the television in the living room. He picked up the other remote for the TV in the kitchen and turned it to full volume on Fox News. The sixty-inch screen in the living room he turned to football. Tanner loved their house remodel. The open floor plan proved to be brilliant. Of course, he would never tell his wife. As far as she knew, he was still bellyaching about the changes. He flipped the switch on the police scanner and heard the police chatter back and forth regarding a stop near the park.

"2015, model Cadillac—license plate BIC 370," the officer said.

What the hell—is that Howard Bone's plate?

"No wants or warrants," the dispatcher announced.

Static filled the air and Tanner strained to listen. "10-4, notify 201," the officer replied.

"10-4—stand by, 210. The chief is on his way to your location. ETA is five minutes. He directed you to proceed."

"Proceed—what in the hell does that mean, proceed?" Tanner picked up the phone and called Donald Armstrong, Attorney. The recorder picked up and announced, "You've reached Donald Armstrong. I'm out of the office and won't be in until Tuesday morning."

Tanner barked into the phone. "Where in the hell are you? Answer the damn phone."

He scrolled through his phone and found Anthony Asmus' number, pushed buttons and heard the accountant's machine pick up. "Damn it, why won't somebody answer the phone? This is Tucker, call me, my number is 646-1912."

Tanner shoved a bite of cereal in his mouth. "Disgusting," he mumbled. "I might as well go to the diner." He left the cereal on the granite island and headed to the garage, opened the door to his new truck, and tried to haul himself into the massive pickup. Failing, he tried again. "Damn, it, what was I thinking, buying this truck?"

He started the pickup and the roar of the engine rattled the tools in the garage. He backed out, swerved and knocked over a garden gnome. "I'll catch hell for that," he muttered. "He was probably her favorite man."

Tanner drove into town and slowed to a crawl at the golf course. He thought he should be coming up on the traffic stop soon. Tanner spotted a police car and the chief's SUV parked haphazardly on the side of the road and he stopped rubbernecking long enough to see the sheriff's car approaching from the south.

"There's that big son of a bitch. Why would he be there if it was just a traffic stop?" Tucker drove past the stop, turned left into the shopping center, and stopped facing the direction of the scene. He could see an officer with a camera snapping pictures of an open trunk. "Damn, I can't see, and why doesn't someone call me back?" Tucker muttered.

An officer led a man in hand cuffs to the back of the police vehicle and another was speaking to a woman. "Is that Melony?" Tanner said.

The officer escorted her to the other police vehicle and helped her into the front seat. Within moments it left the scene.

Tucker searched for his binoculars. His phone rang. Caller ID read Asmus. Tucker yelled into the phone, "Where in the hell have you been?"

"I've been at church, not that it's any of your damn business. I'm on my cellphone, what do you want?"

"What kind of vehicle does Howard drive?"

"A Cadillac, almost like mine, his is white—mine is cappuccino colored. Why?"

"The police stopped a Cadillac, it's pulled over by the side of the road. I think they took Howard to jail."

"I don't give a damn. I'm going home. You don't have any idea what I've just been through. I left Stephanie at church. I may have to go back and get her."

"I'm telling you, somethin's up. I think it has to do with the li'l bitch, Kate Anderson. You need to meet with me, and we need to make sure we have our tracks covered."

"All right. After I tell you about tonight you'll *really* think something's up and—now that I think of it, Howard wasn't in church. I'll come to your office. We've got to get that gal. We've got to get her real good."

The developer was busy watching the police drama unravel and did not notice the black snake that crawled out of the gunny sack on the floor. It slid up the console over to the dashboard and wrapped itself around the steering wheel.

Tanner screamed as he came face to face with the huge snake. He tried to open the door, but it was locked. He finally jimmied the door open and fell out of the truck onto his left hip. The snake followed. Tucker lay on the pavement kicking and screaming like a toddler. "I think I broke my hip. Someone help me! Get that snake off me."

A young man with a video camera captured the entire scene.

๛   ๛   ๛

The accountant was headed home. He pulled a hastily executed U-turn in the road. The vehicle slid on the wet pavement and veered into the guard rail. The rail rattled down the entire side of the Cadillac, smashing and screeching the side of the SUV. The driver over-corrected, veering into the center lane where it was almost hit head-on by a semi-truck. Asmus jerked the steering wheel and avoided a head-on collision, but not a crash. The semi hit the Cadillac in the passenger rear door. The vehicle then swerved across the road, clipped the end of guard rail, flipped over onto its top and slid down the bank into a ravine. The accountant hung upside down, held there by a seat belt.

❧   ❧   ❧

The semi driver drove on, took the next exit, turned the large truck around, and headed in the direction of the crash. She did not see any lights or sirens leaving the small town as she turned the radio up and rolled on. She stopped at the nearest truck stop, swung out of the vehicle and looked at her front bumper. She took the sleeve of her flannel shirt and swiped the smudge of white paint. *Good enough, bug juice will take care of it before I get to Chicago.*

She sat down at the counter—curly brown hair stuck out of her red bandana. She gave the waitress a big grin, "Coffee please—what's your special?"

CHAPTER TWENTY-EIGHT

A PIECE TO THE PUZZLE

K ate stood at the kitchen island, practicing her new skill of cutting vegetables, "chef style," as she called it. She hoped she didn't cut the tips of her fingers off. The class she and Susie took at a local restaurant was fun, but she much preferred to use a paring knife as she was taught as a child.

The mailman shoved a package and some envelopes through the mail slot. Kate dropped the knife, washed her hands, walked over, and picked up the mail. A small package, wrapped in an old brown sack and sealed with duct tape, caught her eye. It had the return address of Warren Epperson, Chula, Missouri.

Warren Epperson, that's Pop's old friend. She pulled the duct tape back and spilled out a disc. *Do I have anything to play this on? I think my computer is too modern to play this.* She turned around the room and finally realized she would have to dig out her old computer. It groaned while it ran through the updates, but Kate was able to push the disc in and hit play.

The video started with Warren Epperson tapping on the video screen.

"Hello. Is that damn camera on? It is? Okay, I'll start."

Warren Epperson, Theodore Anderson's best friend, straightened himself. His white hair, white skin, and thread bare white shirt made him look almost ghost-like. He spoke softly and slowly as if he might be taking his last breath.

"No man should have to tell this story, but I'm not gonna let the sons of bitches get away with it. It killed…plain and simple, it killed him. Losing their farms, his fishing cabin and being disinherited by his wife. But, mostly, admitting to his granddaughter he had been a stupid old fool."

Kate paused the video and stood up, grabbed a Kleenex, and wiped tears from her eyes. She paced around the room. *Pops, you weren't an old fool, you were the smartest man I ever met.*

She pushed play, and the video started again.

"I don't have any pallbearers. Ted used to tell me, 'Aw, Warren, don't worry about it — I'll put you in the ground.' Now, he's gone. Who's gonna carry me now? I sit here waiting until the day I'm gone, like a puff of smoke." The old man tried to snap his fingers, but there was no noise, just air.

"I know I had a life before Ted, but don't remember much of it. They tell me I used to fly a plane for, uh, don't remember his name. Don't remember a thing about it.

"Oh, yeah, uh—the story. The granddaughter, oh, why can't I think of her name? She's a good girl. Theodore was hard on her growing up. He was so pissed when his only son crashed that plane. Then, they couldn't find his granddaughter. Didn't know where to look and when they did find her—well, the kid wouldn't stop talking about her folks. She was so little, with those big brown eyes. Serious like, she would ask when they were coming home. His wife died a broken-hearted woman. He was already in the bottle. Drinking, driving, blowing stuff up. I liked that part. We blew the hell out of tree stumps making that lake. Can't even buy dynamite now. Bob probably has a ton of it in his barn. Son-bitch."

"Sir, you're rambling." A person in the background spoke.

Warren waved at him. "My story, gotta tell it the way it comes to me. Smoking, that's what's done this to me. I would like a good cigar right now. That's what ate up my bones. Course, I liked my booze too."

The old man laughed softly and shook his head, "We would light that fuse with the end of my big cigar and scramble up the side of the dam. Boom!"

"Ted, well, he smoked and drank and prayed. I don't know which vice he had worse. You would think a man would have enough sense not to drink and pray, but not that man—he was a prayin' man—Catholic. Interesting religion, that whole confession thing. All those days you gotta go to church. Ted never missed any of those holy days. Some days, he was drunk—but he went to church—and I suppose he thought that would buy him a ticket into heaven. That, and a lawyer bringing booze and peach pie to the nursing home where his wife was. Who doesn't like peach pie? They couldn't resist the lawyer's charm. Do you suppose they signed papers over alcohol?

"Did I tell you he was my best friend? We built an airplane out there in that barn. He said, 'Warren, order the parts, we'll figure it out.' What he meant—you pay for it, you put it together, you fly the damn thing and I'll drink and smoke and pray. Of course, his boy, right there with us handing me wrenches. I regret the day we ever ordered that plane. Maybe that boy would be alive today. He'd be fifty-some years old now.

A small gasp fell out of Kate and she covered her mouth as tears fell to the floor. She grabbed several tissues and stuffed her eyes. She got up, paced around the room, and cuss words fell like a rain storm as she stomped her feet like a toddler. After several minutes, she poured herself a small whiskey and sat back down in front of the computer screen.

"After we built the plane, Ted married the woman he worked for. She had inherited drug stores from her first husband. They had a marriage arrangement. They went to see her lawyer, got a prenup thing—even though it was her who wanted to get married. Ted didn't want her money. Years later, they decided to combine all assets—went to the lawyer again. Over and over they

201

saw the lawyer. After each tax year the accountant sent them there.

"I told him—don't trust the son of a bitch, but Ted liked being a high roller. He liked being in the country club. I guess that's what rich people do, change their wills. She had some farms, but the farm with the cabin was his. He paid her for it. I would swear by that.

"Anyway, my wife, bless her soul, started losing her brain—Alzheimer's. She didn't know who I was sometimes. She was terrified when I came into the house and she didn't recognize me. I got to thinking, I might die, what would happen to her? We didn't have any kids, so I visited with Ted's attorney.

"We set up all kinds of paperwork, what if I died first, what if she died first. I thought I would give my land to the Conservation Department and a little piece to my neighbor. He was good to us and especially to my wife. I forgot all about that somehow, talking to this feller—this attorney. He told me how valuable the land would be if I left it to the town. The money would be used to build a soccer field for the kids. I didn't have any kids of my own, maybe it was a good thing to do. He said the Conservation Department didn't need the money, they had enough money.

"Anyhow—well, the feller said he would come out and we could sign papers here at the farm. I figured, well, he was a nosy lawyer or didn't have much to do, so I agreed. My wife was having a bad day. She didn't hardly know nothin'. She sat at the kitchen table and didn't bother to comb her hair. I tried to get her to understand we had company coming, but she was having a bad day.

"The lawyer brought all the paperwork. He started his speech and went through his stacks of paper. Twenty pages—he just skimmed through it, adding words like and 'this here is some attorney language' and before I knew it, I was signing the damn papers.

"My wife put her hand on top of her head and felt her hair. I guess she realized she hadn't combed it. Her wits were back, I saw it in her blue eyes. She yelled at the lawyer, 'Get outta my house! We're giving our land to our neighbor and to the Missouri Conservation Department, do you hear me? Don't you come back.' She picked up her plate of bacon and eggs and threw it at him." The old man laughed. "She had a temper and was always pretty good at throwin' and breakin' things. I learned to duck the first year of our marriage."

The old man took a drink of water, looked down, and opened a small drawer in the table. "I've heard other stories about this lawyer who could sell shit to outhouse salesmen. This lawyer who bilked their folks out of their money. I wrote their names down. It ain't right, stealing from the elderly. People who worked their whole life to leave something grand to the world, only to have it stolen from them when they're weak, and old, and confused. There ought to be a law against it. They're people out there sayin' 'Well, it's for the greater good.' Greater good, who gets to decide? Lawyers lining their pockets, that's what it is.

I guess I'll quit my preachin', it's all I got to say."

The computer screen turned black. Kate looked in the package and found a piece of paper torn out of an old notebook. On the paper, scrawled like chicken scratch, were twenty-six names.

Kate picked up the paper, studied the names, and immediately started her internet searches. "Thank you, Warren, this is what I needed! More clues."

CHAPTER TWENTY-NINE

TYING UP LOOSE ENDS

Susie Jones—born Katherine Whittington—lived the life of a little girl raised with a silver spoon in her mouth. The Whittingtons came from old money, but her father and mother had no business skills of their own. The only real skill the two of them had was throwing dinner parties. By the time Katherine reached age fifteen, her parents had burned through most of their inheritances. To maintain their life in Boston, they planned to ride their daughter's future by matching her with a wealthy banker who had money to spare. The banker, John Elliott, was ready to settle down and start a family. He wanted tall, beautiful, athletic kids. Katherine, a natural athlete and nearly six feet tall, fit the bill perfectly. She came from breeding, dressed exquisitely, and seemed to be subservient to her father's demands.

The prospective groom followed custom, treated the parents to the local country club for dinner, and courted Katherine in the old-fashioned Victorian ways. The idea of an arranged marriage appealed to him. He attended

Katherine's tennis matches and loved her little white tennis skirt.

One Sunday afternoon, John said, "Darling, why don't you try to play golf?"

"I'll need lessons, John." He arranged for them immediately. She studied the game, like she did everything in life, with a passion. First lessons showed she had an amazing natural talent and soon she was taking lessons from a pro. This caused some conflict with John Elliott as he wondered how long it would take before she would be beating him regularly at the game he loved so much.

"Hey, John, that fiancée of yours is going to give you a run for your money," men drinking beer at the nineteenth hole would laugh.

"Don't I know it, in more ways than one," John replied each time. The golfers—dressed in all colors and styles—laughed and slapped each other on the back. John didn't care. He dreamed of the day he could take her to bed. He could not wait for her eighteenth birthday. He shopped for dresses and accessories for their nights at the country club. Of course, each outfit came with matching bras and panties.

Bailing the parents out of their financial mess was considered a math problem. Most of it would be done through low-interest bank loans. He would also supervise the remodel of the family home which, of course, would someday be his.

On Katherine's eighteenth birthday, she skipped her graduation and engagement party, cashed in her savings, and disappeared in her red Mustang, her expensive clothes left in the closet. Katherine had picked the car, the one choice she had ever been allowed to make. It did not come equipped with GPS monitoring like the BMW sports car her parents had chosen.

Susie Jones showed up at South East Missouri State College with a full-ride scholarship for academics. She played golf and won enough to make it fun, but stayed under the radar. She studied law enforcement and theatre because she found them useful to her new life. Susie turned running away from home into a game and pretended to be from England. The theatre teacher, a true Brit, helped her with her linguistics.

ও   ও   ও

Today, as Susie drove out to the golf course in Kingseat, Missouri, her competitive spirit dialed in. The last three months had hardened her. She hated the "good ole" boys who reminded her of the country clubbers back home. The voice inside her head kept repeating, "How dare they rob Pops?" It was a beautiful Wednesday morning in late November. Cloudless blue skies kept the sun shining brightly and warmed the air to a nice fifty-seven degrees.

Susie arrived early for a forty-five-minute drill. She took each club and practiced carefully. Checking the distance of each shot with her GolfBuddy, a graph formed in Susie's brain as she studied the layout of the course. She walked over to the putting green and checked the speed and slope of the greens. *I'm ready.* She left her balls on the driving range and entered the clubhouse.

"I understand there's a standing tee time available at 10:00. First eight in gets to play—is that right, fellas?"

"Sure! Join us," a man in the back shouted. The rest of the men chuckled.

"Well, gentlemen, I believe we have a game." Susie stretched in her short polka-dotted golf skirt—her arms way up over her head, fingers laced, her perfectly polished nails wrapped around the club. She swung gently back and forth and tipped back on her heels in a calf stretch, accentuating her major assets to the room. Her tight cardigan sweater bulged in front. When the actress knew she had the audience where she wanted them, she called, "I assume one of you gentlemen will give me a ride," as she jogged through the door.

The men stood with their mouths hanging open and looked at each other. Three of the younger men scrambled and elbowed their way out the door. Her winning chauffeur grinned at her and introduced himself.

"Hiya, my name is Brian Peterson. I'm the greenskeeper here."

"Pleased to make your acquaintance, Brian." Susie shook his hand. "I understand you're the long-ball stud.

Since you've been so kind to be my chauffeur, how 'bout we make the game a little more interesting? How does ten dollars a hole sound?" Susie swung her blonde ponytail and slowly placed a long piece of gum into her cherry-lipped mouth. "I'll play the black tees."

Brian hesitated, took his hat off and scratched his head. "Sure, what's your name, honey?"

"Honey will do just fine," Susie drawled. "Do you think the other boys would like to gamble with me? My daddy sent me my allowance, and I figured I would spread it around town a bit." She batted her black eyelashes at him.

"I'm sure they would love to play - with *you*." He grinned and winked at her, showing off his big white teeth.

"Oh, this is so much fun—what a beautiful day, I just love this little ole town. Look at that big church steeple in the background. Look at these beautiful orange trees. They almost tremble like a woman under a man's touch. Oh, Brian, is there even a sinner in this here little ole town?"

Before Brian could answer, two other golfers showed up on the first tee. They all agreed to play ten dollars a hole.

"You boys go ahead, I'm not quite ready. Hey, do you have a couple guys out this week?" Susie twisted and turned with her driver above her head, stretching again.

"Yeah, one's in the hospital and the other's in jail." The guys laughed.

"Oh my—in jail and in the hospital?" Susie puckered up her lips and shook her head. "Oh, I do feel really sorry for those guys. Naughty of you boys to laugh." She took her index finger and shook it at the men.

"Forget those losers, let's see you hit that little white ball," Brian whispered in Susie's ear.

"All right, sugar." Susie strode up to the tee. Remembering she had an audience, she waggled her club, wiggled her butt, and then turned to the men watching. "Do you think I can out-drive Brian?" The three laughed. As greenskeeper of the course, he was by far the longest in the club. While the men laughed, Susie swung her club straight back and carried through to the ball in a flawless swing. All eyes followed the ball as it hung in the air and fell to the ground in the middle of the fairway, inches from Brian's ball.

The second foursome of golfers pulled their carts up in time to see the shot. One of the men in the second group said, "Hey, isn't she the Dolly Parton from church the other night?"

"I believe it is!" A second man, dressed in Christmas red, yelled.

Susie turned and looked at the balding troll-like figure. "And, what if I am? Does it give you a reason to welch on your bets? I tell you what boys, I'll cut straight to the chase. I have no desire to play golf with your asses and I don't want your money. My name is Susie Jones. Theodore and Helen Anderson were dear friends of mine. It makes me want to vomit the way you've swindled the elderly in this town."

Susie paused for effect. No one spoke. "Reese Matthews is your Chief of Po-lice, wave to him, he's sitting in the parking lot out there." Susie turned and gave Reese a big wave and blew a kiss at him. "I believe you good ole boys messed with the wrong old people." She placed her hands on her hips and the smile left her face. "Perps, you may know this drill. First one who talks receives the 'get out of jail free' card."

Chief Matthews opened his car door and swung out of the SUV. He placed his white Stetson on his head and motioned the men over to the clubhouse. Susie shooed them like they were a flock of geese. "Go on now, figure out your lies, call your attorneys."

For some odd reason, the men headed into the clubhouse like naughty school children.

CHAPTER THIRTY

AN OLD FRIEND

T he office of the Attorney General was in the Capital Plaza government building in Jefferson City, Missouri. It was a constant hum of activity, with paperwork messengered back and forth to the governor's mansion and to the state legislatures.

Bunny Dawkins was bored with it all. She missed field work with Missouri Probation and Parole, she missed Kansas City, and she missed her friends. Her new assignment as an elder advocate was not the job she dreamed she would have at this point in her life, but personal safety was important and she had twins to raise. She picked up her coffee cup and looked at the stack of files on the desk. The phone rang. She grabbed the receiver, "Good morning, this is Dawkins."

"And, this—is Kate Anderson, a voice from your past."

"Get outta here! Kate, how are you? How did you do that? I was just thinking about the good old days."

"I'm great, Bunny. No longer running from the cops, as you probably know. Why haven't you bought my book?"

Bunny laughed. "Outrageous self-promotion! I don't buy books. I don't read—but if you want to send me a free signed copy, I'll consider giving it a look."

"Consider it done. I hope you enjoy it."

"Are you coming to town, Kate? Are you offering to be my chauffeur?"

"Hell no, you couldn't pay me enough to work *that* gig again."

Kate and Bunny met years ago when Kate offered to drive the Parole Board member around Kingseat, Missouri, and set up her recorder at parole hearings in the small prison near town. Because Bunny was pregnant with the twins, she was ordered by her doctor not to lift anything over ten pounds. Bunny's husband, a state senator, had been against Bunny leaving Jefferson City, but he finally agreed when she arranged a driver.

"Just call me your mule," Kate had teased Bunny as she lugged the equipment to and from the car.

"Oh, shut it, driver," Bunny would respond.

Ms. Dawkins, a back-seat driver and control freak, had been a challenge for Kate, but they managed to have some fun even in a small town, with a very pregnant woman. The husband's hunch had been correct. If not for Kate's keen observation and fast driving, he would have lost Bunny and their unborn babies when she passed out in the back seat of the state-issued Jeep Wrangler.

"But, by now you probably know, I want something," Kate said.

"Of course, Kate. I owe you several favors. If I can't help you, I will find someone who can."

"Bunny, it was my job as a safety trainer and my deepest honor to have helped you. Everyone else would have done the same. It's a happy coincidence that brought me to you today."

"Kate, seriously, I will always be eternally grateful to you. And, I doubt everyone would have done the same. You got me to the hospital, stayed with me long after you should have gone home, and dealt with my hysterical husband. Walk in my shoes a bit and you would understand."

"Okay, Bunny, I do understand, but I want your professional opinion, nothing else. I'm sending you a packet of information. It's white collar crime, stealing from old people. My name is involved, so it is different, it's personal. I may not be objective. I'm hoping you will have enough for a joint investigation with the FBI."

"And, my area of expertise, it is meant to be! Nothing's changed, Kate, if you say you have a case, I *know* you have a case.

"I'm hoping you'll refer it to the FBI for a Federal organized crime case. I don't want these guys caught and charged, I want them buried. I think organized crime is still a twenty-year stint.

Bunny sat up in her chair. "You've made my day! I have been so bored. There is a very handsome FBI agent working this area, I'll call him as soon as I hang up the phone."

"I'll plan to come to Jeff City and see you and those growing kids. How are they?"

"They're great, Kate, seven years old now. Tony will be so happy when I text him and tell him you will visit. He's on the Senate floor right now. He likes for me to distract him while he's running the Senate," Bunny laughed and then her tone changed. "We pray for you every night. The kids hold your picture as they pray. You're Auntie Kate to them, even though they've never met you."

"Thank you, Bunny, I'm really at a loss for words on that one." Kate paused for a moment. "I…I better run before you try to save me. I have a deadline for a newspaper article."

Bunny laughed, a big belly laugh. "Kate, seriously, I'm looking forward to this. Send me that file."

CHAPTER THIRTY-ONE

THE END

T he apartment, once sparkling with lights and girly décor, now looked like a storage unit. Labeled brown boxes lined the wall in the living room. A Coach suitcase stood by the front door. The matching purse and a short leather jacket hung on a wall hook.

Kate sat at the kitchen island and drank her vanilla cream coffee out of a blue pottery mug. She looked at the front page of the paper. In the upper center fold, a large picture showed a Cadillac upside down in a ravine. The headline read:

LOCAL ACCOUNTANT INVOLVED IN NEAR FATAL CRASH

Kate flicked the paper and went to the next article.

CHARGES PENDING AGAINST LONG-TIME LOCAL ATTORNEY

She scanned the article even though she had written it herself. The newspaper was one of Kate's new free-lance clients. She received a check for one hundred-fifty dollars for the in-depth story which began, "A firearm stolen from the sheriff's evidence room…"

Inside on the social page, under wedding announcements, another large picture appeared showing a local doctor and his wife, Mr. and Mrs. Terrance Williams. The doctor sat in a wheel chair with an oxygen tube running into his nose, his black bow tie slightly crooked. His beaming bride, Cammie Williams, stood by his side, wearing a strapless wedding gown.

Susie Jones received a hundred-dollar fee for the picture and the accompanying two-line blurb.

In the legal notifications there were several new lawsuits.

Kate Anderson vs. H.O.G.G.

Kate Anderson vs. Armstrong, Knight and Slaughter, Attorneys-at-Law

Kate Anderson vs. the Kingseat Housing Authority

Kate Anderson vs. Kingseat Education Foundation

"You about ready?" Susie appeared from the other room, wearing Wrangler jeans and Stetson cowgirl boots. Her sweatshirt was bright pink and torn at the neck, with white glittery letters spelling the word PINK across her chest.

"Wow, you look…casual. I like it."

Susie twirled like a ballerina. "Thanks. I like my new look, especially since my new boyfriend took me shopping and picked out my entire ensemble. I'm headed to the steak night with my big handsome copper." Susie pointed at Kate. "Is that the same outfit you wore in here three months ago?"

"It's my flying outfit. It worked last time," Kate laughed. "I know, I know, you think I need to update my wardrobe. These are last year's style. I'm not a shopper, never will be."

"Interesting articles in the paper tonight, you might want to read them. I guess what goes around comes around," Kate said.

"Cheeky, Kate. You know I will meticulously cut them out and place them in your scrapbook. I love to cut and paste. How'd the picture of Cammie and the Doc turn out?"

"It showed a beautiful beaming bride. You're not still doing scrapbooks old-school style?"

"Yes, I don't know why, because you have your digital portfolio and your scrapbook. You never look at either of them so why should I care?" Susie pouted. The pout only lasted a second before she launched the question. "Your new pen name, J.J. Clarke, work for you? Do you like the byline?"

"I read an article this morning on Facebook. I understand it's vogue to use a grandmother's name."

"Only because you wrote *it,* too!" Susie laughed. "I'm going to miss you, Kate. I love your dry wit."

"Oh, stop it. It's only going to be a week." Kate changed the subject. "The Kingseater will be a nice addition to our portfolios—they don't edit a word and they take my advice on the photographs. It will be great bread and butter for our business."

"We all like bread and butter and pie and cheeseburgers and food, especially here in Missouri." Susie hugged her best friend.

"Speaking of the bread and butter, Susie, have you put on a few pounds? Is that the real reason you're wearing that sweatshirt?"

"Shut up! Back to business. I love my first published picture, it tells such a great story."

Kate placed the paper towel roll to her mouth as a pretend microphone. "A hard-working nurse gets involved with a dream boat doctor who is also her boss. But then—she finds out he's been drugging his elderly clients. In fact, drugging them to death! And…he and his gang of thieves steal their money. The nurse is heartbroken until she finds out the doc was planning to dump her and she meets the heroines of the story, who unravel the crime and make the bad guys pay. Not happening to *that* Missouri Girl."

"A new twist to the Cinderella story."

"Or, the beginning of a coffee-table book."

"Kate, stop—business, business. All business makes you incredibly boring. Stop thinking of projects, go down and meet your handsome bloke by the curb like you're anxious to go with him."

"Do you think she gave him Trazodone?"

"Looks like it to me." Kate shrugged. "Couldn't have happened to a nicer guy. Are you sure you don't mind finishing the packing by yourself?"

"Don't be silly. You need to get away. It will be fun, I'll have lots of help, and besides—it's almost done. I'll see you in Tampa in ten days."

Susie's mood turned. She put one hand on her hip and pointed a finger at Kate. "Just because I'm dressed like a farmer doesn't mean I'm ready to settle down—and neither are you. Let's promise we won't end up like a Hallmark movie."

Kate swung into her jacket and hung her purse on her shoulder, "You mean the Hallmark movie where a snotty big city girl stays with the small-town handsome Chief of Police? It's not too late to keep this apartment."

"Or," Susie said, "the movie where a small-town girl comes home to help an elderly grandfather and winds up flying off with a handsome bloke to Hawaii."

"It sounds like a Hallmark movie to me."

"Pops would love it."

EPILOGUE

Mark Larsen, the new accountant, stared at the tax document, the last IRS filing for Theodore Anderson, deceased. *How can a man's finances plummet from the 32% tax bracket to below poverty? The poor old bastard still tithed to the Catholic Church. I hope he got a ticket to heaven.*

Howard Bone spent a few days in jail, arranged bail and now awaits trial for possession of a stolen weapon. The Sheriff's Office has not been able to tie him to the murder of Robert O'Dell.

Anthony Asmus survived the car accident and is in a rehabilitation center in Columbia, Missouri.

Doctor Terrance Williams and Cammie live in Las Vegas, Nevada. The doctor is homebound, but Cammie is seen at local casinos and live shows with a man who resembles Doctor Williams' pilot.

The Kingseat Housing Authority resigned its not-for-profit status. The proceeds were distributed to the Catholic school as per the settlement agreement from the lawsuit filed by Kate Anderson.

The Missouri Attorney General's Office opened an investigation into organized crime. The investigation resulted in eleven search warrants for local businesses.

After ten days in Hawaii, Kate and Susie returned to Tampa where Susie planned a big roll-out for Kate's second book, *Dared to Run*. The Vlog business was sold to Amy and Emily. Susie is a frequent visitor of Kingseat, Missouri.

Kate is writing her third novel, *Meet the Serials*—a book about the murderers she interviewed while she worked for the State of Missouri.

QUESTIONS AND TOPICS FOR DISCUSSION

1. Have you ever met someone on a plane and kept in touch?

2. Pops is part of "The Greatest Generation." He hides information from Kate and winds up hurting himself. Have you experienced someone like this?

3. Kate believes the H.O.G.G. Accounting Firm robs her grandparents. Do you know someone whose inheritance has been stolen?

4. Pop's doctor prescribes Aricept for dementia without giving him any tests. Do you find this to be a believable story line?

5. Friendship is key to this novel. Would you want to hear more about Susie?

6. Is Reese Matthews, the handsome "copper" in the story, a good guy or a bad guy?

7. There are no legal remedies for Pops, but Kate takes matters to the extreme. Were there other things she could have done instead?

8. Do you know the difference between a will and a trust? Do you think your affairs are in order and your wishes will be carried out after you die?

9. Who was the truck driver who ran the accountant off the road?

10. Traditional cozy novels begin with a murder. Are you disappointed there was not a murder?

ABOUT THE AUTHOR

J. J. Clarke, author of Dared to Return, spent her career in the State of Missouri as an investigator, parole officer, and district administrator. She also sat on the Parole Board, and writing concise, factual reports for the courts system was an important part of the job.

After marrying her husband Barry Johnson, she wrote grants and assisted in developing a not-for-profit group that obtained and restored The Tillman House, an historic landmark museum in Brookfield, Missouri.

Clark began writing *Dared to Return* when her parents became ill and she left her museum work to help them. She praises her writer's group for encouraging her to continue to write and develop strong characters with dynamic dialogue.

"I hope my book is entertaining and thought-provoking. I wrote it as an escape and for book clubs—a short, weekend beach read with topics for discussion that promote engaged conversation."

Clarke's first book in the Kate Anderson series, *Dared to Run*, tells the story of Kate as a young parole officer who is stalked by a deputy sheriff. Rated five stars by Chanticleer Reviews, *Dared to Run* has "action on every page as Clarke quickly sweeps the reader into Kate's perils."

All books by J.J. Clarke are available on Amazon.

She loves to hear from her fans. Please contact her at jjclarkeauthor@gmail.com.

Made in the USA
Coppell, TX
25 October 2021

64625975R00142